WHERE MONSTERS PRAY

STORIES

TRISHA J. WOOLDRIDGE

WHERE MONSTERS PRAY

STORIES

TRISHA J. WOOLDRIDGE

PINK
NARCISSUS
PRESS

Where Monsters Pray
© 2024 Trisha J. Wooldridge

Many of the works in this collection have been previously published, as follows:

"The Mass of the Greatest Sin": *Wicked Weird,* NEHW Press, Aug 2019. "At Least the Chickens are All Right": *The Twisted Book of Shadows,* Twisted Publishing, Oct 2019. "Better Horrors and Gardens": published with alternate title in *Poetry Showcase: Volume VIII,* Horror Writers Association, Nov 2021. "Heart of Frankenstein": *Wicked Creatures,* NEHW Press, Oct 2021. "Mary Shelley's Baby": *Nothing's Sacred Volume 4,* Jack of No Trades Productions, Oct 2018. Reprinted in StokerCon 2019 Anthology, Horror Writers Association, April 2019. "Turnpike Mary Answers Prayers" : *Paranormal Contact: A Quiet Horror Confessional,* Cemetary Gates Media, March 2021. "Fixed": *Corrupts Absolutely?: Dark Metahuman Fiction,* Damnation Books, March 2012.

Cover design and illustrations by Michael Takeda

Published by Pink Narcissus Press
Massachusetts, USA
pinknarc.com

ISBN: 978-1-939056-22-1
First trade paperback edition: June 2024

CONTENTS

For Scott,
Husband-of-Awesome,
who introduced me to the best monsters,
"I'm so glad you're evil too."

For the Mary and her beloved monster who changed
the world for speculative fiction.

CONTENT WARNING

This work includes
misogyny, racism, ableism, diversified bigotry
to women, children, men, *queers*—
the word "queer" is used—
and pigmented persons also referenced by ethnic slurs.
Harmful stereotypes are presented as the norm.
This work contains rape and violence—
without consent, obviously, but sometimes with.
Consent is unclearly depicted; sexual descriptions are vivid,
graphic, chaotic, and messy.
In this work,
women, children, men, teenagers, cis and transpersons,
elderly, and nonbinary folx die;
people of all skin pigmentations die.
No one is safe, but some die at a higher rate than others.
The cat dies. So does the dog and the horse and the rabbit.
The chickens live—
they're evolved dinosaurs after all.
This work includes references to evolution.
God-Goddess-Nonbinary Deity exists and doesn't exist.
God-Goddess-Nonbinary Deity is dead.
Religious zealots kill people.
Religious zealots save people.
This work contains problematic depictions of religion.
The government does not have your best interest in mind.
The government commits genocide to maintain power.
This work includes genocide and controversial

representations of governing bodies.

In this work,

mental illness is frequently villified, occasionally savant or holy, and also gendered;

morality and ethics are presented as biological, ethnic, and gendered;

portrayals of self-harm and suicidal ideation are portrayed as reasonable responses to reality.

Put down the book, leave the theatre, adjust the settings of your electronic device.

Close your eyes.

The content is still there.

This work of horror is life.

THE LAST UNICORN SACRIFICE
IN NEW HAMPSHIRE

THE LAST UNICORN SACRIFICE IN NEW HAMPSHIRE

Emily choked back a gasp when she saw the unicorn in the church courtyard. It was far from the first time she'd seen it; in fact, if it *didn't* show up for too long, the parishioners started to worry.

But this time it looked *wrong*.

Tildy, Emily's best friend (and maybe more), did gasp.

"You haven't seen it before, have you?" Emily's mom whispered, patting the other girl on her shoulder. "He's a messenger from God. He works for the angels. That's how we know *this* is the right path for us to follow." She said the last part with a knowing nod to both Tildy and her father, who sat next to them on the pew. Tildy's mom wasn't there; she went to a Catholic church in Fitchburg, Mass. Tildy and her sister, Mia, normally went with her.

Tildy leveled her fear-wide eyes at Emily.

She sees what I'm seeing. Emily gave a tiny nod and a smile her friend would know was fake but their parents would think was agreement. She turned to her twin sister, Beth, whose face gave nothing away. Frustrated when Beth didn't even look at her, Emily accidentally-on-purpose fumbled her Bible-sized hymnal and dropped it on Beth's foot.

Beth didn't even glare.

She must see it too.

When Emily picked up the heavy book, she jostled

Beth's elbow.

Beth started singing "The Church in the Wildwood" as the organ chords signaled the chorus.

Feeling Tildy's look, Emily glanced at her. Her friend mouthed, "What the…?"

"Later," Emily mouthed back, opening the hymnal with a shake. The pages fell to the well-worn hymn.

Tildy followed Emily's lead and began singing.

"Oh come, come, come, come

Come to the church by the wildwood…"

Despite this being only Tildy's second time at the church, she carried the tune well and Emily found herself just listening to her friend's beautiful voice, watching her lips rather than singing herself. As the chorus ended and the choirmaster/organist took over, Emily chanced a look outside again.

Her stomach twisted. It was still there, prancing in a circle. Bone white. *Wrong.* Jagged hooves. *Wrong.* Sharp horn glimmering in the sun. *Wrong. Wrong. Wrong.*

Emily didn't wonder *why* the unicorn looked different; she wondered *which* "why" had caused the change. Had changed her.

Yesterday had been hers and Beth's thirteenth birthday, and she had sinned. More than once. With Tildy.

***

Most people thought The Church of the Sacred Horn referenced the angels' trumpets in the Book of Revelation. The parishioners—the True Believers, not those who occasionally visited—knew better. Reverend Thomas B. White had been given a vision made flesh of a heavenly beast who brought the prayers of the faithful to the angels.

A unicorn.

In return, they were asked only to be faithful, follow the Word of God as the Reverend preached it, and to make a single sacrifice every Easter—no more than what God had done for his Chosen.

When God was pleased with their work, His love and preference was apparent. The parishioners could see it in brilliant, holy pure-white and gold. After service and after Sunday school, on days the unicorn visited, they could touch the holes in the ground from its cloven hooves. Proof of their covenant with God.

Tildy and Mia went to the general Sunday school after service. Emily and Beth went to the "advanced" class they'd been selected for when they were ten. Tildy gave Emily a tortured look upon their separation that was only part joking. Emily did her best to give Tildy an "it'll be all right" look, but she wasn't sure how convincing she was. Lying was also a sin, so she might just be making the situation worse in wanting to assure her friend (and maybe more, which was also a sin).

Tildy had moved to the town of Blessed Waters just after Emily and Beth had started their "advanced" Sunday school. Since starting the program, Emily learned what it meant for their town to be blessed with its unicorn. God had promised his Chosen Few a world without illness, strife, war—and Blessed Waters was a piece of that world on earth, proof that such a thing could exist because He willed it so.

"Advanced" Sunday school was only for seven girls, selected when they turned ten, and while it explained a lot of things—like how almost all the adults in town had really good, well-paying jobs; how kids never got sick; how pets never got lost; how the local farms always had good crops and the cows always gave plenty of milk and chickens always laid plenty of eggs year round—the class didn't explain why it was always all girls. Emily had asked about that, since Jesus was obviously a boy and Elijah had been asked to sacrifice his *son.*

Deacon Jim—he shared teaching the class with Mrs. Esther White, the Reverend's wife—had told them that the message the original Reverend White (the current Reverend White's great-grandfather) had said that it had to be pure, virginal women who were called to the unicorn. It had been so for hundreds of years, perhaps thousands of years, that such a covenant existed. One could find proof of that in the old medieval tapestries where a virgin was given to a unicorn or, among the Unfaithful, used as a lure for a unicorn by men who wished to steal God's power. The unicorn was a most holy messenger who could travel between Heaven and earth, and therefore could only touch the purest sacrifice to God. The touch of the impure would sicken the unicorn, kill it even.

"Why can't virgin boys be the purest?" Emily had pressed. That's when the Deacon had grown red and reminded her that she was bordering on sinfulness by questioning the Most Holy Word.

Emily didn't want to be sinful or go to Hell, but she had been doing a lot of questioning since Tildy had moved in. She knew if she said anything, Tildy would be called "an agent of the Fallen One" for making Emily question and they wouldn't be allowed to be friends (not to mention "maybe more," which was a BIG sin anyway).

The seven girls easily fit into the Reverend's office for this class. Little TV tables were scattered by the couch, the cushy leather and plush chairs, and the few folding chairs that made a circle in the center of the room. Whoever was teaching would usually walk around the room.

As they walked through the windowed hall from the main church to the Reverend's office, Emily saw the adults setting up the folding banquet tables and chairs in the courtyard. It was the first nice Sunday after a long winter.

Only, they were all moving slowly, looking toward the main church doors...

Emily turned a choking gasp into a cough.

The unicorn was still out there. It was *never* out there after service where regular people, where *sinners*, could be so close. The other girls noticed and stopped to stare.

The other girls' faces beamed only unbridled delight and awe. Their eyes shone and their lips opened into wide smiles.

They don't see what I see...

She looked for Beth and barely caught a glimpse of her twin walking alongside Deacon Jim before he and Mrs. Esther shooed them from the window to the office.

"Be respectful! We're being honored. Reverend White is being honored. Come now!" Mrs. Esther gave Emily a shove that she thought was a little harder than necessary. When she looked at the woman, she half-expected to see another monster revealed, but no. She was as perfect looking as always—though this close, Emily could see the little lines around her eyes and lips that immaculate "peaches and cream" makeup did not entirely hide. Tildy had once showed Emily a video of a makeup tutorial for the "all natural" look Mrs. Esther strove for—and it was a lot of work to look like someone didn't need makeup!

Emily tried to weave through the group to get to her twin, but Deacon Jim had an arm around Beth's shoulders and had sat her in one of the office's floral-and-stripe patterned wing chairs that made it hard to sit next to someone because the armrests and backs flared out so much. Still, Emily maneuvered around to grab a folding chair—she *hated* the folding chairs; her butt always hurt after sitting in one for the whole two-hour long class—and set it up next to Beth.

"You saw something different today," she hissed while

everyone else was still chit-chatting around finding their seats and trying to sit next to their closest friends.

Beth furrowed her brow at her in confusion. "What do you mean?" she whispered back.

Emily blinked. What if Beth hadn't seen the difference? What if she were reading her twin wrong? They had been drifting apart since being selected for "advanced" Sunday school—since Tildy had moved in, Emily also had to admit. What if it *were* just she and Tildy who were seeing…a distorted unicorn…because *they* had been the ones who'd sinned?

Deacon Jim tapped his forefinger on Reverend White's shiny, wooden desk. The lip around the top was a spiral that resembled the unicorn's horn, the namesake of the church.

"We are only one moon cycle away from Easter, girls," he said.

Emily didn't want to be reminded of that.

"How are you all doing?" Mrs. Esther asked. "Are you being good? Are you praying for your souls' protection?"

Emily nodded a lie.

"Good, because as we get closer, the Fallen One is going to approach you all." Deacon Jim was using his sermon voice. "You won't realize it. He's a clever one, a smart one. He was an angel once, after all. He tricked God's first Chosen Ones—the purest first, for the corruption of the most pure is what he craves most of all—he will come for you because you're Chosen, you're special, you are who God wants in his Kingdom. You need to be always vigilant, for he'll come as your closest friends, as the sweetest boys who will tell you that you're beautiful and special. You mustn't let them in, for even the smallest trespass destroys your purity. Remember, your promise of Heaven, of being rejoined with your family and loved ones in pure bliss, is what's at stake.

"And the health of this town, of your families, of the people you love—their life on earth as well as their chance to get to Heaven—depends on you. Depends on you being worthy to kneel before the unicorn as a gift to God."

Emily tried not to shake, tried to breathe normally even though her chest felt like it was being squeezed by a giant hand. *I'm going to Hell. I could make other people go to Hell.* She'd known that before this moment, but she felt like she *knew* it even more as the Deacon said it.

It's bullshit, she heard an imaginary Tildy say in her head. *God is forgiving. He doesn't send kids to Hell.*

She didn't believe Tildy was Satan in disguise or one of Satan's servants. That didn't feel *right.*

"We have what no one else has on this earth, a living, breathing servant of God looking after us. We are the Chosen Ones, and we are bound by a special covenant *directly* with our Holy Lord. You, you were chosen especially for this honor. One of you, on the back of the unicorn, will be delivered directly into the House of God to protect our sanctity while we still walk this sinful earth."

"Amen," they all murmured, even Emily.

"And we know it hasn't been easy for all of you. There is much pleasure in this world that you are all forsaking..." When they had been chosen, they had vowed to protect their purity more than the other kids. They'd promised to never see a movie not approved by their parents and the church, not to read a book outside of what was in the church's library, not to wear "clothing for men" like jeans and T-shirts, and certainly not to wear any skirt or dress or blouse that was immodest—particularly as they'd begun to develop into women. Mrs. Esther had given them *plenty* of talks about *that.*

"So, let us pr—"

Reverend White burst into the room. "It has been

revealed! Who among you is the Chosen! He has revealed it to me today!"

Despite the bitterness burning up her throat and the painful beats of her heart, Emily couldn't help but sit straighter and smooth her skirt like the rest of the girls. They all had perfect enough manners to not spit out the question fluttering on all their lips.

He looked around the room, resting his gaze on no girl longer than any other before bowing his head and holding out his arms. "The Good Lord blesses us every year, all of us, and gives honor to one of our congregation to be brought to Him early. It is not easy to be a Chosen One of God, so let us all open our hearts, give strength, and pray for…Elizabeth Wilson."

Emily mashed her folded hands to her mouth not in prayer but to keep from puking.

***

Emily wasn't getting anywhere near her twin. Her own twin. Reverend White flanked her on one side, and Mrs. Esther and Deacon Jim seemed to be competing for who got to put their arm around her other side. The rest of the class dissipated into the crowds, each finding their respective families in either relief or dejection for not being the Chosen One. The rest of the congregation surged toward the front doors to offer their prayers and thanks to God, the unicorn, and Beth.

"What is going on?" Tildy demanded, wrapping her arm around Emily's.

Emily shook her head. She couldn't tell Tildy. Every so often she'd felt sick for not telling Tildy about the biggest thing in her life, about being Chosen by the church and what it meant—but they were all forbidden from talking about it to non-baptized, non-confirmed parishioners of Church of the Horn.

"Can we go?" Emily choked out over the taste of bile.

"Don't you want to be here for your sister, for whatever honor she's getting?" Tildy looked confused.

Emily shook her head, then stopped, pulling away from Tildy. "Just…meet me at my house?" Words flew from Emily's lips before she realized what she was saying. "Bring your bike."

Tildy hesitated, but nodded and left. The church was only a few blocks from their houses.

Glancing over her shoulder to make sure no one noticed her slipping away, she headed home. It was even more difficult to keep from running than it was to keep from puking.

★★★

"Are you going to tell me what the *fuck* that thing was outside your church or not?!"

Emily was fighting the blur that was trying to overtake her vision. It was all she could do to keep pedaling her bike, to keep moving. She hadn't said a word to Tildy since they'd left her house.

"Don't—don't use words like that! When you talk about…about…" She clenched her jaw shut as she felt her bike waver.

"Seriously? Emily!" Tildy stood up on her bike and pumped herself several lengths ahead of Emily, then turned sharply in front of her and braked.

"Hey!" Emily's voice squeaked as she clutched her breaks and slammed both her feet down, scuffing her good Sunday shoes.

"Talk to me! Please, Emmy, you're freaking me out. Like for real. Please, please just talk to me? I'm-I'm scared."

Emily blinked, taken aback at Tildy's confession. She came from Fitchburg, which had gangs and all sorts of crime and awful things, and *she* was scared? *She saw what you saw,* Emily reminded herself. *And that ought to terrify anyone.* "So am I," Emily said back.

"So tell me what's going on. What happened today? What was that at your church? What's happening to Beth?" …

Emily took a deep breath. "Remember how your mom says you can't take communion at our church, and if I went to yours I wouldn't be allowed to? It's like that. I-I can't tell you because…because…that."

Tildy pressed her mouth so tightly her lips almost disappeared. She took several deep breaths through her nose. People did that, Emily had noticed, when they didn't want to yell. Tildy spoke in that I'm-calm-and-not-yelling voice. "We just saw…what looked like-like a *monster,* a *demon* at your church during mass-service-whatever you call it. We saw that. That happened. And you can't tell me what it is?"

"It's the unicorn." Emily knew Tildy was aware that a unicorn protected the church, so she could say this much without breaking the rules.

"That did *not* look like any unicorn I've ever seen. And it certainly didn't look like it came from *God.*" When Emily didn't say anything, Tildy pressed. "I *know* you saw what I saw. You looked scared. Really scared."

Emily took a breath. "That's not what it normally looks like."

"You've literally seen this unicorn before? It's a real unicorn?"

Emily nodded. "It's…it *was*…beautiful." What she and Tildy had seen that morning was *not* beautiful.

Tildy looked down at her bike. Everyone was still at church, so there were no cars. "It doesn't…normally look… like it did today?" she asked softly.

"No," Emily said, running her finger over the pink

ridges on her bike handles.

"Did it...? Do you think it looked different today... because we...you know?"

"I don't know. Maybe. Or it could be..."

"Because we visited that creepy stone?"

"Yeah..."

Tildy looked in the direction they'd been riding. "That's where we're going now, isn't it?"

Emily hadn't thought about a direction when she'd grabbed her bike, but after Tildy said it, she knew that was where she was going. She nodded.

"You know you had nightmares last night. Like bad ones." She took a breath. "I thought it was 'cause, you know."

"It was the rock," Emily said.

"So why are we going back?"

"Because...because...I *have* to. Please?"

With a sigh, Tildy got back on her seat and started pedaling. And while Emily couldn't help but notice how the ruffles on the bottom of her flowered dress rippled in the wind, she also noticed Tildy's back and shoulders were as stiff as boards.

★★★

Yesterday.

It was the first sleepover the twins had ever had or been to. The rest of the "advanced" class had been invited, and Emily had begged for Tildy to join them—even though that meant the other girls would have to "be careful" with what they talked about. Tildy had had to beg her mom, too, because Mrs. Anderson (Mrs. Sanchez-Anderson, but Tildy said her mom didn't feel comfortable using her whole name in the town) had started taking Tildy and Mia every weekend to visit her family and go to church down in

Fitchburg.

The other girls were scattered around the room with air mattresses and sleeping bags. Except for Beth, who was in her top bunk, alone. The other girls had been avoiding even sitting next to Tildy all night and laughed at her beat-up My Little Pony sleeping bag, the only thing she'd brought to sleep on. Emily, annoyed at all of them, had scooted all the way over in her bed, till her back was against the wall, and invited Tildy to join her. Some of the girls had looked at her funny, but Emily had quoted, "'Tell me then, who was really this girl's neighbor?'" Paraphrasing the Good Samaritan parable shut them up. She didn't consider most of them friends, anyway.

But having Tildy in her bed…Well, Emily had never slept next to anyone except Beth. Tildy was taller than the twins and, even though she was only a few months older, she *looked* older. More developed. And she smelled different. Like far away beaches and roasted chestnuts.

"Everyone else is asleep," Tildy whispered. "We win for staying up latest."

Emily giggled and nodded. Behind Tildy, on Beth's desk, glowed a pastel crystal cross on a cloud with bunnies and lambs, an Easter gift when the twins had been Chosen at ten, after their confirmation. It cast a rosy, rainbow halo around Tildy's head and revealed the slumber of the other five girls. Someone ripped out a fart that sent her into a snorting snore. Both of them covered their faces with the blanket to keep away the offending stench and smother their own laughter.

"So, did you get everything you wanted for your birthday?" Tildy asked when it was safe to peek back out of the blanket.

Emily thought for a moment. She hadn't really wanted much for her birthday except for Tildy to be included in the party. At the same time, there was a lot she *wanted*. She wanted to read any book she could get her hands on. She wanted to not feel guilty watching cartoons and Nickelodeon shows at Tildy's house when they were doing homework (before Tildy's dad got home from his job). She wanted to do all the things she was not supposed to do as a Chosen One...In her head, she recited that list with Mrs. Esther, Deacon Jim, and the class.

"That look on your face tells me *no*, you didn't get everything you wanted."

Emily shrugged, trying to push the chant of thoughts from her brain. "Nah, it's fine. It's sinful to want things."

"It's your birthday, though. Even Jesus got gifts on his birthday. What's one thing, more than anything else, that you want?" She twisted behind her and grabbed her phone from the nightstand. "Look, it's only eleven-fifty-two. Still your birthday." She flipped her thumbs over the screen then held up an animated cake with a candle. "Make a wish."

Emily couldn't help but giggle again. She blew at Tildy's phone. As she did so, Tildy swiped the screen and the candle silently exploded into streams of ribbons and a floating "Happy Birthday!"

"What'd'ja wish for?"

"Aren't you supposed to keep your wishes secret?" Emily countered, though her heart hammered a challenge all the way up to her head.

"Only from parents, not best friends," Tildy stated. "Eleven fifty-five. You're running out of time for your wish, Emily Wilson."

"A kiss," she blurted, then covered her mouth. Where had that thought come from? The stupid list. Though, the list specifically said kissing or touching *boys*. Still...Face on fire, Emily closed her eyes and forced her hands from her mouth so she could hiss, "Sorry...sorry...I..."

Tildy kissed her.

Tildy kissed me!

It was soft and tasted of toothpaste and felt *really nice.*

Emily opened her eyes wide so wide it took a second for Tildy to come into focus.

Tildy wore a smile that begged *don't hate me,* and squeaked, "Happy birthday?"

After curling her lips over her teeth and running her tongue over them to taste the kiss, Emily grinned the biggest smile she ever remembered feeling and mouthed "Thank you," because she now understood how a kiss could make someone breathless—and you needed breath to speak.

Tildy let out a big sigh. A fresh smile showed her pretty lips more and crinkled the edges of her long-lashed eyes.

Emily edged a little closer, and her hand found Tildy's under the covers, and they laced their fingers together. Still unable to find words, she tilted her head more, leaning toward Tildy, brows up in a hesitant question.

Tildy leaned her head more toward Emily, silently asking the same.

Emily gave a tiny nod that Tildy mimicked as they drew close enough to touch lips one more time. This kiss was not much longer than the first little peck, but it felt even better. It felt nice well past Emily's lips and face and chest and...

"We should probably go to sleep," Emily said when she found enough breath to speak. "Church in the morning." That everyone would go to church together was one of the selling points the twins had pitched to their parents for having a party.

"Yeah, you're right." Tildy scooched further under the covers. Emily did the same. Neither let go of the other's hand.

***

As they leaned their bikes on a pair of trash trees far from the road, Emily thought of Tildy's hand holding hers. In the nightmare, she'd felt like she was being pulled out, pulled to safety. Yet she woke up gasping, as if suffocating —which at least had kept her from screaming and waking anyone else up. Tildy had been whispering her name and saying, "It's okay. It's just a dream," and clutching Emily's hand.

The two faced each other awkwardly, each fluttering a hand toward each other, and then finding something to fix on her dress or a reason to reposition her bike.

Swallowing hard, Emily walked away first. "They're gonna wonder what's wrong if I'm gone too long," she said. The sensation of frost prickled inside her chest as she caught the flicker of hurt on Tildy's face.

After a huff of breath, Tildy's footsteps padded in the winter-softened blanket of leaves, crunching remaining piles of icy snow. "So why did you need to come back here? Yesterday and today?"

"I...I just did." The words were sour yogurt on Emily's tongue.

"That's not a good reason. Not a *real* reason. It's like our parents saying ''Cause I said so.' It's bullshit."

"If you don't—If you don't want to come with me, you can head back." Those words felt cold and slimy, too.

"Excuse me?" Tildy did stop, her voice lilting with that "ghetto" attitude Emily only knew from television commercials, the only other place she'd seen Puerto Rican people before meeting Tildy and her mom.

Emily kept walking as tears burned her eyes. It was probably better to make Tildy hate her. She couldn't tell Tildy about being a Chosen One, about Beth being *the* Chosen One, and what that meant...or what the unicorn meant or maybe why he might look like a monster to their eyes now. It was stupid of her to have made friends with someone outside of the church. It would have been easier if she just kept to herself, like she'd done for years. But when Beth started getting popular with the other church girls, when Deacon Jim paid her the most attention—was that why she was *the* Chosen One?—Emily had felt so alone. And she'd felt bad for the new girl sitting by herself in the lunchroom while Emily was feeling overcrowded at the *in* table next to her sister.

Tildy had liked books, too, and fairy tales—the stories Emily wasn't allowed to read anymore. When Beth had found Emily's secret collection of books and threatened to tell on her, Emily had given them all to Tildy. She wasn't allowed to read them anymore, but the chanted "don't" rules didn't include hearing someone talk about them.

Just like the rules never mentioned kissing *girls*.

But Emily knew what wasn't being said. Knowing the difference between what was said and what was meant and what got included in the rules was the key to most of the fairy stories—how the kids outsmarted the witches, trolls, and ogres.

She didn't hear Tildy walking anymore. One of the videos Tildy had showed her—the rules hadn't said anything about YouTube videos on a friend's phone either! —said that black holes were heavy things with a lot of gravity. It was an accurate description of how Emily's stomach felt—heavy, empty-but-not-empty, and getting heavier.

It's for the better, she assured herself as she continued walking the path.

The rules *had* explicitly said no wandering in the woods. No exploring, hiking, or camping without an adult.

Both Tildy's parents worked long shifts and had long commutes, but Emily had failed to mention that to her parents. Since Tildy had a phone (something she said was "normal" for the kids in Fitchburg) and could text her mom any time, Emily's parents had just assumed Tildy's mom was at home. Cities were dangerous—anywhere outside of Blessed Waters was *dangerous*—so they understood why other parents would want their child to have a phone and check in with them.

Tildy had wanted to explore when they'd started hanging out. Emily had held out for almost two years. Just over a year ago was when Tildy's parents had started arguing, so when Tildy had said, "I just need to get out of the house," Emily had gone with her. That's when they'd found "the place with the creepy rock."

The "creepy rock" was a flat rock with a ring on it—the kind that people chained things to. It was in a clearing surrounded by white birch. On the other side of the clearing came the sound of water running, like a large stream, but neither girl had yet crossed the clearing. That first time finding it, both had thought they "heard something" and had run back to their bikes after just two steps beyond the birches.

Last night was not the first nightmare Emily had had about that clearing and creepy rock. She never told anyone about her nightmares, though, and Beth had never said anything about hearing Emily wake up screaming or anything.

Tildy and Emily had gone back to the stone once before. It had been Tildy's idea because she missed "doing spooky stuff" for Halloween. Halloween, as Emily knew it, was a holiday for Satan. After Tildy spending days trying to explain to Emily otherwise—*her* church celebrated saints and deceased family members around Halloween—she'd finally accused Emily of being too scared to return to the rock, which was *obviously* haunted or where something awful had happened since it was so creepy. Emily had felt the need to prove herself. The two had gotten halfway from the edge of the clearing to the rock before they "heard something" and ran back to the bikes again.

As they got closer and closer to the Easter after their thirteenth birthday, Emily had felt the need to go back to that clearing. That's why she'd begged Tildy to go yesterday. Emily's parents had been busy planning for the party and appreciated Emily "staying at Tildy's house"; Mr. Anderson had been happy to hear his daughter was "helping out" one of the other church families. Deacon Jim had asked for Beth's help in preparing for Sunday's service, so she'd gone to the church, upholding her reputation as "the good twin."

Emily stood between two birches and stared at the flat rock. Sunlight reflected tiny dimples of water in its surface. It looked almost pretty.

Long yellow grass bent in pillowed waves as it tried to stand after months of snow weighing it down. A few spots of white still sparkled around the clearing's edge.

Emily shook like the few golden leaves clinging to their trees. Her feet, cold and wet because her patent leather Mary Janes weren't waterproof, planted her in place. Gusts of wind came from different directions, carrying different smells. Sharp, icy water from one side, decaying leaves and a dank stench from somewhere else, a breath of ash from another direction.

Yesterday, she had walked all the way to the center of the clearing, to the creepy stone and its ring. The ring looked solid, not rusty but still old. The rock was a blue-grey granite that looked like it ought to have been smooth but had many deep gouges tinged reddish-brown. Yesterday, Emily had edged her foot through the tangling grass and touched the tip of her boot to the stone while Tildy had stood behind her—conceding that Emily was the braver one and saying she felt something *wrong* about the whole place. *Wrong* like the unicorn this morning.

When the unicorn visited the church courtyard, when the weather was nice outside, its hooves tore up the grass in deep gouges.

Emily didn't remember walking over to the stone this time. One minute her knuckles hurt from griping the trunk of a birch, the next she was at the stone looking at the divots and grooves that weren't all that different from the church's lawn after a unicorn visit.

"You know what's really creepy? I don't even hear any birds—"

Emily yelped, jumping in surprise at Tildy's voice. Her Sunday shoes slipped in the wet grass, tangled, and she fell on her hands and knees on the stone.

***

Knees ache. Arms ache. Wrists ache. It's cold, so cold and so hard. Dampness seeps through a soft white dress or nightgown…nightgown, nothing else. Shivering, shivering.

It must've rained the night before. Puddles on the stone are bigger.

That's not my face in the reflection.

There's breathing, sniffing, snorting. Getting closer.

I know that face.

Looking up from the reflection, see it. Just like the last time. Wrong. Its face, his face, is white skin stretched over an elongated skull, fraying silvery lines at the joints. Pale green eyes drip silver and black lines from sunken sockets. Tears? The eyes are too hard and cold for tears, and they have those horizontal pupils like goats and pictures of the Devil. Gotta look away.

I know that face too.

The puddles show a different reflection in each. All wide-eyed, all pale, all shivering.

Clack, clack, scrape.

Jagged two-pronged hooves—also like the Devil has, but also like old unicorn paintings and tapestries—step onto the stone, send ripples through the puddles. Hooves are silver and black. Broken. Legs are bones and muscle and sinew and silver veins. Unicorn blood is silver. Even the muscle is white. Flaps of matted white fur and skin are the same color as bone. Skin hangs like a cape over the shoulders and down the unicorn's back. Beneath, white ribs ring around moving, pumping organs.

Clack, scrape.

Closer. Puddles ripple. A hot wind—the unicorn's breath—smells of rot and sulfur and strokes cheeks, flutters fine blonde hair into eyes where it scratches, blurs vision.

My hair at least.

The puddles' ripples slow and the other faces of the other girls, all Chosen Ones, each start to scream, twist in pain. Red swirls and stains the puddles, and then pain and—

***

"Emily! Emmy! Say something. Please, just say something?"

Tildy was holding her up. They were by the bikes. Emily had no recollection between falling on the stone and getting back to the bikes. She was shaking and gasping and her face was sticky with tears and snot. Tildy was muttering something in Spanish and touching her forehead, chest, and shoulders. She looked very pale.

"Emily?" she asked again, voice rough.

She just nodded and pressed a hand just below her stomach where it felt like she was twisting inside. Like when she got *that time of the month*, but worse.

"What happened? You just started screaming..."

"You were right," Emily whispered. Her voice scraped her throat like when she'd had strep throat a few years ago.

"There's something really wrong with that place."

"Did you...did you see something? Like a vision?"

Emily swallowed hard, though it hurt. "It's...a blur. And-and I don't want to talk about it. Can we...can we just head back?"

"Sure. You sure you can ride?"

Emily took a shaky breath. "Maybe we can just walk our bikes for a little bit?"

"Yeah, we can." Tildy took a deep breath. "Emily?"

"Yeah?" She squeezed her eyes closed. There was nothing Tildy was going to ask that she wanted to answer.

"Are you okay?"

No, she thought, but wasn't going to say that. "I will be," she said, knowing that answer was also a lie.

Tildy moved one hand from her handlebars to cover Emily's and squeezed. When she took it back to hold up her bike, Emily was both saddened and relieved.

As they walked back in silence, Emily sorted the pain and images into three conclusions.

That place and the unicorn were tricking her church and not from God at all.

If the place and the unicorn really did work for God, she no longer wanted anything to do with God.

There was no way she was letting anyone bring her sister to that place and give her to the unicorn.

***

Beth and Emily were identical twins, but not the kind that would trade places to trick people. Even if mischief and pranks hadn't been so frowned on in the church, they weren't generally given to such behavior. Elizabeth had declared she was "Beth" when they were four because she had thought it was silly their names began with the same letter.

Emily studied Beth all month and realized she didn't

know nearly as much about her twin as she thought. Beth was quieter than Emily'd always figured. She didn't say much at school or even at lunch. The other girls, particularly the "Chosen Ones" who now could enjoy more normal lives, still followed her around, but she was never *part* of them. If *they* noticed, Emily couldn't tell. She also felt awful not knowing if *the* Chosen One Beth was acting differently than any-other-time Beth.

How had they grown so apart? When?

She did notice that while Deacon Jim definitely gave Beth preferential treatment, Beth didn't seem to like him near her. When she'd asked about that odd fact, Beth pretended she didn't know what Emily was talking about. And although Emily could still tell when Beth was lying, Beth also seemed to have known that Emily knew and had asked if they could just do something nice together since they only had a little time left before Easter. Emily couldn't say no to that and had spent an entire Saturday playing every board game in the house with her twin.

As difficult as it was counting down until Easter, making her plan to keep Beth from being put on that rock, it *felt* harder to push Tildy away. Emily would be cold, and then Tildy would find something funny or kind to say, and she'd be laughing, forgetting about the awfulness of a monster unicorn and...doing whatever she would have to do. (She hadn't quite gotten past the "don't let Beth be taken away" part of her plan, even though she knew *something bigger* had to still happen or next year someone else would be on that rock facing a monster.)

Finally, it was the Thursday before Easter and Tildy was sitting on the bus looking like she'd been crying.

"What's wrong?"

"They're finally doing it...getting a divorce," she said softly, slouching.

Emily slouched beside her, feeling sick. "I'm sorry."

"They were up fighting all night. Mom left for work this morning with a suitcase telling Dad he better bring me down to her family for Easter after I'm out of school, but I know he won't. And if anyone from Mom's family comes up to get me, he'll call the cops. You think the cops 'round here aren't gonna listen to whatever a white man is saying about some 'Puerto Rican thugs'?"

"They know your mom, though..."

"Yeah, but she's stuck covering four full shifts till Sunday morning. There's, like, five nurses out on maternity at Leominster State, where she works, and *everyone* wants Easter off to be with their family. She'll be lucky to catch four hours of sleep on the couch between shifts. She can't drive all the way back up here to get me."

"I'm sorry," Emily said again. She squeezed Tildy's hand and found herself unable to let go. *Bad idea!* she scolded herself, to no avail. They hadn't done anything outside the realms of "just friends" since the sleepover.

"I'm sorry to unload on you. I know you got things hard with your family, too, with whatever's going on with your sister and the church and all." Tildy laced her fingers through Emily's. She gave a little snort. "I guess I'll see at least part of it. Not like Dad's *not* gonna make me go to church."

Emily's stomach flipped. *Tildy can't be here!* She'd been counting on Tildy not being around. If she were here, especially for the Saturday dinner, she'd want to hang out and Emily had to be focused. She knew her plan wasn't great—sneak a bunch of powdered sleeping pills into her sister's food, get her to fall asleep in the bottom bunk, and pretend to be her on Sunday morning—but having Tildy around was a thing Emily hadn't planned for!

Emily snatched her hand away from Tildy. She had to be

awful, and she had to be awful *now.* "Do you always have to insult my church so much?" she snapped.

"I'm sorry. I didn't mean to—"

"Yeah. You did. You think we're some weird cult because you don't want to believe that we're the only ones going to get to Heaven!"

"Excuse you. What the *what* are you talking about?"

"I'm talking about you knowing that you're going to go to Hell and trying to drag me with you!" Emily scooted toward the windows as if disgusted even being near Tildy. She'd seen the other girls be that way, so she knew how it looked. She closed her eyes and pictured the unicorn's boney face and Devil-pupil eyes so she wouldn't have to see the hurt on Tildy's face. Her heart literally felt like shattering glass, its pieces tumbling into her churning stomach.

She heard the smallest squeak from Tildy before her spring jacket scraped against seat vinyl as Emily felt her stand up. She listened to her sneakers pat toward the back where there were more empty seats, and then reminded herself what all the screams of all the Chosen Ones sounded like to keep herself from crying.

***

Saturday, the church had its big dinner honoring Beth as the Chosen One, their direct envoy to God through the unicorn. Tildy was there with her father and not even looking at Emily, which hurt but was for the best. The twins had gotten their Easter haircuts Thursday night and Emily managed to get an identical cut and style to Beth's.

Her mother had looked like she'd been fighting tears when she drove home from the hairdresser. Her father had been strangely silent upon seeing the haircuts when they'd gotten home. Beth, for all her "not going to be *that* kind of identical twins," had said that it looked good and had hugged Emily long and tight before they left the hairdresser. Since Emily had never been close to any of the prior Chosen Ones, it hadn't occurred to her how difficult it was for even the families to get near their daughters. Beth sat at the head table between Reverend White and Deacon Jim. How was she going to get near any of Beth's food?

As the night went on, Emily got more and more frustrated. Her mother kept pulling Emily into hugs, even holding her on her lap, for the whole dinner. She wore a lot of makeup that didn't hide the red rings and puffiness under her eyes. Their father seemed cold, hardly wanting a hug from either of his daughters or his wife. Emily couldn't tell if he was angry or just trying very hard to not look sad. After all, Beth being *the* Chosen One was an honor. (Emily lost count of how many times that had been said at the dinner.)

When dessert was over and people were getting their coats, Emily found herself gripping the chair. She hadn't gotten close to Beth at all! The tiny baggie of broken sleeping pills that she'd stolen (she was going to Hell anyway, what did it matter?) from the Rite Aid was still hidden in her bra.

Was there ice cream at home? Perhaps she could put an ice cream dish together for Beth when they got home?

Emily's stomach lurched for an entirely different reason…no, not her stomach, lower…like something from dinner wasn't agreeing with her. She excused herself to the bathroom.

As she headed there, a dizziness set upon her. Fighting not to slip on the tiles in her new Easter shoes, she leaned on the wall, which was cold and hard—not as fuzzy as it looked. Just a few more steps.

"It'll be all right. Trust me." Deacon Jim's voice echoed in her brain. He was leading Beth to the rest room, too.

As he just about carried Beth into the single stall bathroom, he gave Emily a look that sent a different sickness shivering through her.

That was the last thing she remembered.

***

She was cold. Her knees hurt. Her arms hurt. Dampness seeped through thin material that was the only barrier between her shins and a rough surface.

Emily blinked her eyes, realizing they were already open but unfocused. It was still dark outside.

She gasped. In the distance, she heard human footsteps getting softer as they swished through dead leaves and crunched on remaining snow piles.

There were no birdsongs. The sound of water rushed not too far away.

She was here instead of Beth…but how?

And now what?

Her heart hammered as she listened for the sound of four jagged hooves, snorting, anything.

When she was eight, the Chosen Ones started the "Advanced" class at thirteen and one was given to the unicorn at sixteen. Then something had happened. They said the girl, Mary had been her name, hadn't protected her purity well enough. People got sick that year, the only time people got sick. Others lost their jobs. There were accidents. People started getting tainted water from their wells. After that, they'd started "Advanced" classes at ten and given girls at thirteen.

Deacon Jim and Mrs. Esther had said that impurity hurt the unicorn, could kill it. Had that been what happened? Why it was awful now?

As she knelt on the rock, she knew that was untrue. The unicorn had always been what it was. Whether it was her "impurity" or having touched this rock, something just let her and Tildy see it. The question was if "impurity" really did hurt the unicorn and if she was "impure" enough to destroy it.

Her wrists were handcuffed, and the chain of the cuffs went through the ring on the stone. Emily gave a few good tugs, but the chain held and the ring was embedded deep. Fighting against the panic her heart was beating out, Emily tried to think of what she could do. If she was going to stop this, stop the unicorn, she'd have to...kill it. And as much as she could list her sins, she wasn't sure they were enough. Even though the Reverend said any sin on one's heart could send a person to Hell, Emily's heart said there were definitely worse sins than others. And if Mary, at sixteen, hadn't killed the unicorn by just being "impure," there must be more.

There wasn't much slack to the chain around her wrists; she might be able to wriggle herself to her feet, but she would still be bent over in just a white nightgown. She couldn't even leverage the nightgown like a rope with her hands bound down. Could she kick hard enough to do anything? Probably not against a monster with a sharp horn and sharp hooves.

A hot wind rustled her gown and the grass around her. It smelled of sulfur and rot, old meat and metal on a hot day. Emily shivered and looked around.

The clearing was lit by pre-dawn light that only barely separated shadows from darkness. A swishing crinkle of leaves sounded deliberate steps. Not human ones.

Directly in front of Emily, across the clearing, the unicorn emerged from the trees.

She made herself stare at it. At its *wrongness*. The stretched, torn, matted fur and skin. Crusty silver and black surrounded the long pointed bone of its horn. Instead of the perfect spiral of paintings and tapestries, it grew like a branch—still pointed sharp at the end. Lines of fine silver spread and wrapped like veins.

The sickly green eyes glowed in the dim light.

Emily took a deep breath. "What are you really?" she demanded.

The beast paused, one unevenly pointed hoof off the ground. It tilted its head as if considering her, but said nothing. It opened its mouth, flaring tattered lips as it took a deep sniff of her, and then snorted out several times. It continued its approach.

"Hey! I'm talking to you!" Emily could either panic or be crazy; what else could she do? She yanked her wrists to no avail. "If you're going to kill me, I want to know why! I don't believe you work for God!" *Yank. Yank.* She yelped as the cuffs dug in. "I believe you've been tricking my church for years!" *Yank.* The chain was so short! *Yank.* "Are you going to say anything for yourself?"

The unicorn had paused again, snorting loudly. It hopped a few times on its front legs. Bones and tendons creaked and rattled with each movement. Between its ribs, Emily could see its heart beating faster, its lungs expanding and shuddering with each snort.

It ran at her.

Screams cut from the woods. A rock smacked the unicorn's flank. It skidded into a turn and reared. Its tail, mostly bone with a few tufts of fur and matted hair, crackled as it flicked. Another rock hit its chest.

Emily looked in that direction and saw Tildy—*Tildy?!*—just inside the clearing with an arm full of rocks, hitting the unicorn with almost every throw. Emily vaguely remembered Tildy saying she used to play softball back in Fitchburg. It reared again, mouth open as if screaming, but no sound came out, just the hiss of air as its lungs pumped.

"Emmy, shh!" Beth's hand pressed to Emily's mouth to

make sure the instruction was followed.

"What…?" she whispered when Beth moved her hand and started fiddling with a big set of keys, trying them in the cuffs.

"Father Jim switched us. I knew where he kept the spare key chain," was all she said as she tried key after key.

"Why?" Emily asked, dumbfounded.

"Because…" Beth let out a curse Emily would have expected from Tildy as a sixth key still didn't fit. "Because I'm not a virgin and that would mess things up."

"Wh-what?"

"Damnit!" Beth dropped the keys. They *kerchanked* on the rock.

The sound of beating hooves stopped. Both twins looked up. The unicorn looked right at them. It reared once more and ran at them.

"Hey you goddamned fake, super-ugly Queen Chrysalis wannabe!" Tildy screamed, throwing more rocks.

The unicorn ignored her this time.

Beth was trying key after key as fast as she could.

"Raaaaaaaaahh!!" *Thud.* A growled stream of Spanish.

Both looked up. Tildy had run right into the unicorn's side. She clung to the ribs and shoulder as the monster spun, trying to gore with its horn.

"Its heart! Can you reach its heart?" Emily screamed.

Tildy just screamed.

"Leave me the keys! Just help her!" Emily begged her twin.

Beth pressed the heavy collection of keys into Emily's hand and ran to the other side of the unicorn. Another of the unicorn's silent screams hissed through the air upon Beth's touch. It reared, flailing its hooves and throwing Tildy aside. Beth, toes dangling on the ground clung to two ribs. One hoof hit her and she cried out. Blood stained the side of her pajamas.

"Shit, shit, shit, shit," Emily muttered. Trying to use keys while cuffed was harder than it looked. Worse, she couldn't tear her gaze from the unicorn, her sister, and Tildy. She was trying to find the right key and get it in the lock by feel alone.

Blackness crept from Beth's hands over the ribs. When the unicorn landed, the leg that had kicked her—also decayed black—split and burst like rotten fruit. Its fall knocked Beth to the ground. She clutched her side, gasping.

Tildy lunged again, this time with a pointed stick.

The unicorn circled until Tildy was between it and Beth, then ran—stumbled—toward Emily again.

"Don't you dare!" Tildy followed, gasping.

The unicorn jumped entirely off the ground, kicking both rear legs at Tildy and hitting her square in the stomach. She flew back and landed, crumpled, on the ground.

"No!" Emily screamed, dropping the keys.

Another "No!" in the same voice echoed closer. Beth jumped against the unicorn again. Her blood smeared its shoulder, red turning to black and eating at the gaunt flesh. It hopped again, and then tried to sidestep away, falling on its one front leg. Beth ran at it once more, her hands red with her own blood, now staining the entire left side of her pajamas. The blackened ribs bent and split. She reached for the beating heart.

The unicorn curled its back, writhing, kicking. Jagged silver hooves turned black as they tore Beth's pajamas and stomach. Her hands grasped the heart. The unicorn rolled all the way over, pinning Beth.

Emily felt around the rock for the keys, gasping for breath.

"Here," Tildy breathed beside her. The keys clinked as

she took Emily's hands.

Beth's knees bent and pulled; that was all Emily could see of her. The unicorn jerked and snorted. Blackness spread over its lungs and heart. Red wriggling amidst darkening silver veins could be Beth's hands.

The unicorn rolled again, tried to stand. Blackened rear leg bones bent, unable to lift. It fell on Beth's legs. Emily heard her cry out; she could only see her twin's shoes. The unicorn's decaying body was between them. Rot ate at the beast's shoulder, exposing darkening sinew and bone. The unicorn threw its head up in a last agonized, silent scream, then thrashed. Beth started a scream that hung ragged in the air.

"Beth!"

"Got it!" Tildy said.

The cuff dropped from one of Emily's wrists. She tried to stand, but the open cuff caught on the ring. Tildy maneuvered it free, and Emily ran to the unicorn and Beth.

"Oh G—" She stopped herself before saying His name. She fell to her knees.

The unicorn's horn cut through Beth's neck. It stuck there. Black crawled from Beth's blood and the horn started to bend.

Emily shook her head, pressing her hands to her face. Strangely, she couldn't find tears.

"Dios mio!" Tildy fell to her knees next to Emily.

"Fuck God," she whispered back, a fire rising in her chest. "He let this happen. Or he made it happen. Either way, *fuck* Him."

"You don't mean that," Tildy whispered, making that cross gesture she said her church did.

"I do. I really do," Emily growled.

Tildy didn't argue. Emily didn't take her hand when she reached for hers.

The unicorn's horn bent more, breaking. Beth's body collapsed on the grass, her blood staining the yellow waves orange. The unicorn's head fell at a twisted angle. Black liquid from the disintegrating organs stained Beth's pajamas.

Emily scrambled to her feet and shoved the body off her sister. It was lighter than she'd expected, a husk. Grabbing Beth's arms, she dragged her sister out of the spreading black of decay. She sat in the grass and cradled her twin's head in her arms. Tears still didn't come.

Tildy sat next to her. "She killed it. No one else has to die like that," she whispered.

Emily took a deep breath and let out a ragged breath as she combed Beth's hair with her fingers and closed her empty eyes. Tears stung but didn't fall. "How were you even here?"

Tildy swallowed. "I...I was going to return the books you gave me because...because I figured you hated me. I wanted to do it before my mom came to pick me up 'cause I figured I wasn't going to come back here any time soon. I saw Beth—I thought it was you until I saw her take her bike —run out of the house and start riding, so I followed and caught up to her.

"She told me everything. *Everything.* Including..." She swallowed hard again. "Including what Deacon Jim did to her..."

Emily hugged her sister's body tighter. *Why didn't you tell me?* she asked silently, even though she could think of a few answers.

"...And she asked me to help her break into the church, steal some keys, and save you. Of course I said I would. And, well..."

"I was going to take her place anyway," Emily said. "I had a whole plan...and then I got sick last night. And I don't remember anything after that till I woke up here."

"She told me Deacon Jim had drugged both of you, switched your dresses in the bathroom...she remembered that much. She figured he must've told your parents something like 'the Chosen One' having to spend the night at the church or something because she woke up alone in your bunk and you weren't there and your parents were asleep. So she ran out to save you and end the whole unicorn sacrifice thing." Tildy sniffled. "She figured what Deacon Jim had done to her was so bad that if she just touched the unicorn, it would hurt it enough for us to kill it."

A sob choked up Emily's throat. Tears finally came. She didn't push Tildy away when she wrapped her arms around her.

She didn't know how long she cried, but when she finally caught her breath, she whispered, "Now what?"

Tildy adjusted herself and pulled her cell phone out of her back pocket. There were several missed calls and texts from her mom. "I had the ringer off. Figured it wouldn't help in hunting unicorns. I call my mom and have her come get us...and...I don't know...let her figure out stuff after that. She's my mom, she..." Tildy trailed off and looked away.

Emily also looked away, thinking of her mother's hidden tears. Hidden tears and acceptance that her daughter was being sent away as a sacrifice. "Can I stay with you? I...I can't go home."

"Of course. My mom would probably make you, actually, when she hears about this."

Feeling another wave of tears, Emily sucked in the snot dripping from her nose, wiping it with the filthy sleeve of the nightgown that wasn't hers. She didn't want to drip on Beth's face.

Tildy stood to call her mother. She was half bent over, limping. One arm folded over her stomach. Blood and dirt streaked her torn shirt where the unicorn had kicked her. "Mama?...No, I'm not fine…"

Emily looked back at the unicorn's body. The wretched heap of decay no longer even resembled the monster. Would there be anything left to show Tildy's mom? What would she even say?

Emily didn't want to think of that now. She hugged Beth's body once more, kissing her forehead. She'd sacrificed herself for Emily, for future years of girls who would be the unicorn's victims…Deacon Jim's victims…the church's victims. The last sacrifice.

"Thank you," she whispered.

Emily would make Tildy's mom believe her. She would tear the church and this whole town apart if she had to. It'd be worse than when the "impure" Mary was given to the unicorn. Beth had given everything—and that was the purest sacrifice Emily could think of.

She'd make it matter.

THE UNICORN AND THE OLD WOMAN

The old woman on the stairs saw it all.
    She saw it all.
She knew who the dark visitor was.
She saw him in her high, intoxicated, dreamy and drugged
    State of Mind.

She saw him take the children, the babes—
    little ones born addicted,
    abused, abandoned in the ten-story North End
apartment in the city that declared bankruptcy three years
ago.
    Little ones born in that hospice, that Hell;
    Babes born with no hope, save death.

The unicorn came, dressed in the clothes of man,
    Came to steal the babes
    Before they couldn't see.
    Before they said
    -I don't believe-

But the old woman could see him.
The old woman who
    babbled from her newspaper home on the landing
between the fifth and sixth floor of the decrepit ghost-house
apartment.
The old crone with forgotten respect
    and a black, wire rat's nest of hair beneath a dirtsmoke

grey kerchief
    eyes sunken into a coffee-brown skull,
    queenly mantle the essence of old pot and cheap
booze.
She could see the unicorn.

She was magnificent.
    Once.
    Never.
Sleeping Beauty found rest in a pinprick.
    The old woman found Hell.
Her wrinkled hand shook the silver spoon—
    aluminum clad theft from a cafeteria sometime,
somewhere.
The needle kissed the spoon's edge—*clickety-click*
    like a fairy
    tap-dancing
    on a teacup.

Thump on the step.
    She recognized his footfalls by now.
Thump on the step.
    -Why don't you throw away those damned books and
work like your brother?-
Thump on the step.
    Closer.
    -You think you're some kind of princess, do you?-
Thump on the step.
    Closer.
    The pin-prick needle dose made her a princess.
    Lie back.
    Forget.
    Believe.
Thump.

A crone shouldn't drop her special potion.

Tommy Cooper this time,
    not that she looked.
But peripheral vision
    saw the nappy brown-black hair,
      and arms still chubby and dimpled.

Because she did not look she did not see
    the glance *he* cast
    when *he* passed.

Kids in the building
    run down stairs
    and laugh maniacal giggles of childhood's wake.
Kick the old woman.
Throw broken bottles.
    -Points if you get her in the head!-
    -Points if you make her bleed!-
The unicorn would not come for them.

The unicorn came for the last time
    that night.
The crone knew he would not return
    and cried.
She didn't know why,
    just that he wouldn't
    ever again
    evermore.
She cried and
    beneath tears
    found courage.

When his foot touched her filthy landing,
When his foot came near,
She reached to touch
    his suit-coat hem—
    hemorrhaging woman, sinner, who dare not look to
her Savior's face
    but reaches, touches
    the hem
           of His cloak.
She, the sinner, was bleeding.

The unicorn stopped.
    In his arms Jenni Cano,
    three-year-old from the seventh floor,
    who regarded the woman curiously
    now,
    and when her Mami put her outside
    'cuz Papi came home drunk again.
    She looked so happy in the unicorn's arms.

-Yes?- the unicorn asked. The unicorn spoke
    to the dirty and crazy old woman who lived on a
landing, in newspapers,
    squalor,
    waste—
    broken syringe at her knees.

She dared
    cast
    a tiny glance.
    Cinderella peeking from the filthy floor
    to see
    the duke carrying magic-glass-slipper Freedom.

She saw.
He was one of them, all along. That's why he came.

The old woman, the crazy old woman, grabbed his leg
     And sobbed.

-Please, oh please, sir!
I know you. I see you. I know what you do.
I still remember the stories.-

The unicorn-man-beast
     said nothing.

-Make me a child again. I will change.
     I swear.
     I will make better decisions this time around.-

-I cannot unlive the life you led.
     I cannot undo what you have done.
You over estimate my power.-

-But I can see you!- the old woman cried.
-And I have not forgotten.-

The beast in human clothes was touched,
     she saw,
     but still, he shook his head.
He placed the child, Jenni, on the stair
     to address the crone with full attention and proper
dignity.

- I cannot undo what you have done.
     I cannot save you.
     You must do that yourself.

If you can see me, then there is hope.
    That is the only gift I can give.-

-What hope is there for a woman
        too old to climb the stairs?
        Born in hell, raised in hell, kept in hell?
        There is no hope for me!-

Beast entirely, enraged,
        the unicorn reared.
The old woman ducked from
        razor sharp, cloven hooves
        spiraling above her head.
A hazy picture
        of man, of ebon monster unicorn
        fading in and out—
        a withdrawal nightmare real
        and ready to pierce her heart.

-Forgive me- she begged.

-If you will not take
        my gift of hope
Then take
        my gift of death.-

She did not move.
The old woman,
        the frightened crone
        wanted to run away
        but forgot how.

Little Jenni Cano,
        child upon the stair,

watched.
She understood
what the old woman did not.

Spiral horn, a needle
    pointed at the old woman.
Candle-flames danced on the horn, under it
    into her skin
    when he pierced her mortal flesh.
It burned to purify.

It hurt.
She felt a pleasure
    she thought lost,
    like vinyl 45s and *The Bunny Hop* in tap-shoes of Ma's
pans
    that never happened but she saw in an old friend's
fuzzy reel-to-reel projector.
She felt swirling. She felt dancing. She felt hot. She felt
cold.
She felt nothing.

No one in the apartment building noticed
    any noise.
    Or that the old crazy woman was gone.
Not that they noticed before, of course,
    -Turn away. Don't look. Pretend she's not there.-
Nobody remembered
    the babbling hag
    from the landing between the fifth and sixth floor,
covered in dirt and cheap beer,
    surrounded by needles,
    spoons,
    and globular candle ends.

No one recalled
    the three-year-old girl
    who saw a woman who used to be her mom
    get hit by a man who used to be her dad.
    That couple they all whispered that
    —Thank God they never had any children—

And if you asked,
    there never was
        a little boy who stole storybooks to read
        to a baby that screamed through paper-thin walls.
    There never was
        a little girl who knew the boogeyman was real;
        he snuck into her room, at night, in her step-father's
clothes.
    There never was
        a baby thrown into a trash can,
        that child more bruised than not.
The ones the unicorn took
    That never really were.
        Except at night, when you roll over
            to look at what you thought was there.
        Or believed was there,
        in the shadows
        between dreaming and awake,
        between what is and what's said.
        In the drug-induced vision and the vision that cries
to be drugged.

It wasn't really there.
Of course not.
    Because unicorns aren't really there, either.

THE MASS OF THE GREATEST SIN

THE MASS OF THE GREATEST SIN

She didn't expect the tiny tentacle—or arm. It moved too quickly for her to identify if it had suckers.

Arms have suckers on the whole thing; tentacles have suckers only on the end, she reminded herself. Also, *Fuck you, overactive imagination.*

No matter how many times she blinked, she still saw it —that coil, snapping in and out like her nail was some trapdoor. And she'd felt it.

During her freshman year of college, her family had won a trip to Hawaii. It had been their first vacation since she was a child. At an octopus farm they visited, one of the babies had wrapped around her finger. A tiny, curious squeeze—the smallest hug. Octopi were smart; researchers and keepers shared stories about their empathy. Recently, some article suggested cephalopods had alien DNA.

She pulled out the memory of that tiny hug every so often, whenever she needed it.

Like today. It was Monday and time for her annual physical. She'd had to take the T because her car was in the shop.

"Move, you fat bitch." The laughter hurt as much as the words.

Her face burned like the bile in her stomach; the burning enhanced, rather than competed, with the pain of squishing against the unforgiving pole and handle of the seat row's end.

As the three guys laughed, they spread across the four

seats making up the bench. The guy beside her kept rubbing his leg against hers. Laughing each time, making it clear she was taking up too much space.

It was the worst sin: to be a woman and fat.

The unwanted touching, the humor of touching *someone like her*, that was her penance.

Only freaks took pleasure in touching *someone like her*. Chubby chasing was a taboo fetish, an episode's plot point on every fucking police procedural or courtroom drama. *Fat* wasn't normal. *Fat* shouldn't exist.

Every train seat, bus seat, and doctor's office chair bore that truth into her flesh.

Her car's front tie-rods had needed replacement. The mechanic said they'd worn out early, sometimes caused by poor weight distribution in the car. That sounded like bullshit, but she didn't know any other mechanic. She'd given him the money—or rather her not-quite-maxed-out credit card—and resorted to taking the train.

Her parents lived an hour away; it would have put them out to ask for a ride.

They would have asked her how much weight she'd lost since last time they spoke.

She didn't remember the last time they spoke, but she knew no number would be good enough. Not while her ass was so large.

Tuning out cutting laughter, she brushed around the crescent of her forefinger's nail, longing for that tiny cephalopod hug over the hungry churn of her stomach, the embarrassed burn of hot tears, the pinching pain of shoving against a metal bar to lessen the disgusting tingle of unwelcome leg brushing leg.

It's just in my head. What was the point of imagining an impossible act of miniscule affection? It didn't belong, didn't fit in the real world. *Just like me.*

***

The nurse called her name.

She trudged to the scale, gallows-bound. The nurse creaked out a *hrm* like a dropped noose.

The johnny she wore didn't close in the back. She couldn't even tie the string around her hips. Its starched pastel blue showed off every goddamn roll. The sleeves bound her shoulders and the chest squashed her breasts. She had T-shirts from high school that fit better.

Do these not come any bigger or do they purposely give me too-small sizes to remind me how fat I am? she thought. *Or is assuming such malice giving them too much credit?*

The doctor sighed impatiently as her patient shimmied half-out of her johnny so the stethoscope would fit.

"You gained three pounds since your last physical," she noted. "You do know how much damage that does to your heart? Your overall health?"

No, I don't, she wanted to snap. *I forgot since I put down the waiting room magazine with five weight loss ads, four weight loss articles, and three weight loss medication advertorials listing side effects like death and uncontrolled bowels—because smelling like shit and dying are better than being fat.*

She said, "I've *been* trying." She didn't mention her aching joints, the nausea, the exhaustion, the feeling of knives carving her uterus every month. She already knew the prescription. *Just lose some weight.*

"Well, what have you been trying?"

She rattled off the brands of her meal-replacement shakes, how she only ate salads when she did eat lunch, how she had cut out red meat and only ate the whites of hard-boiled eggs. She drank her coffee with skim milk and zero-calorie sweetener.

"Are you getting out? Are you exercising? Are you sure you're not snacking without thinking?"

"I park on the far end of the parking lot, I go to the gym on weekends, and I don't keep any food around to snack on." She imagined her little octopus friend reaching out from under her nail and strangling the doctor.

"See if you can fit in more aerobic exercise, two to three times a week, and check food labels. A lot of so-called health drinks have hidden sugar and fat. And make sure you're getting enough protein…"

All of these things were already written down, reminders taped around her house, folded around the card she used for grocery shopping.

"Let's do a blood test for your sugar. Obesity leads to diabetes, you know."

I had no *idea about that either.* She didn't narrow her eyes or glare or let meanness color her congenial response of "Sure." It was bad enough to be a fat ass; she dare not be a fat *bitch.*

The wait for blood tests took nearly two hours. She was lucky to catch a train and get her car before the shop closed. The blood test's deductible would be on top of losing a whole day of work instead of only half and that was on top of the cost for replacing her tie rods.

The mocha sundae meal replacement shake (nineteen grams of protein and only fifteen grams of sugar) gave less comfort than her imaginary cephalopod friend.

★★★

That night she dreamed of floating, weightless in oceans of darkness where there were no mirrors. The waves' caressing silence gave no reflection and carried no judgement. She was embraced by…something. Anything.

She was loved.

Many arms and tentacles, tiny and large and real,

hugged her and meant it.

When her alarm woke her, her eyes itched with dried tears…

And her arms and chest were covered with reddened circles that looked like sucker marks.

Probably bedsores from so much weight, she reasoned in her doctor's clinically sterile voice.

Still, she found herself caressing each fingernail edge. Disappointment settled in her empty stomach when nothing touched her back.

Leaving the house to get into her newly-fixed car felt like trying to walk out of the ocean. A riptide tried to pull her back to the depths of sleep, where she could contentedly drown in her dreams' siren songs.

Sirens are thin and pretty and don't want a fat octopus-friend. They'd laugh musically at her silly dreams without bothering to curse her with passionate madness.

"Even your daydreams think you're worthless," she muttered to herself.

***

The new chairs at work were "ergonomic." Or rather, they were ergonomic for "normal-sized" people.

Her ass hung on either side of the seat—squeezed out like dough between unyielding arms and curvature.

Given land-leg freedom, Hans Christian Anderson's little mermaid had walked on razors. But she had been thin and pretty and could have fit in an ergonomic chair. Fat thighs offered more meat for the razor-sharp return of sensation upon lunchbreak freedom, and she floundered on boneless octopus legs. The mermaid got off easy—even in the end, where she died and turned into seafoam.

She gratefully slouched, legs uncrossed and unsqueezed, in the non-ergonomic lunchroom chair. She ate alone in a far corner, uninterrupted in counting her twenty chews of wilted lettuce that would supposedly save her life.

Once I've lost weight, I can look for a new job. Everyone knew fat people didn't get hired as easily as thin and pretty people. At a new job, the thinner and better version of herself would be social, have friends, and make more money because she could focus on her career instead of dedicating so much fucking time to losing weight.

She stared at her salad. Oil and vinegar spiraled into green-black holes studded with tomato-seed stars, blurring with liquid viscosity. The unintentional alien beauty behind uninspiring salad was mesmerizing, hypnotizing...

Hypnotism is an ineffective weight loss method. Or at least, it had been ineffective for her.

She poked her fork against her plate, dimpling the dressing and transforming the black-hole swirls into many sucker-puckered arms, wrapping around each other. A giant, otherworldly hug.

"Hey!"

She jumped at the voice and tap on her shoulder. *Blink, blink.* The image of her salad-art tentacles, looking solid and real, hovered over her vision as she tried to focus on the human communicating with her.

"You all right?" Mark from sales—that was it.

"Yeah, fine. Sorry." She blinked again, eyes going to his arms.

Mark worked out every day, or so she'd heard. She'd also heard that he wore a smaller-sized shirt to show off his arms.

Her shirts would hang on him like a tent.

"So, you might want to finish your dessert and get to the quarterly," he said, offering an awkward smile. "Jennalise is on the warpath." His tone was not unkind.

"Uh...okay. Thanks." She looked back at her plate.

Leftover lettuce, too-old tomatoes, smears of olive oil and balsamic vinegar. No art, no alien arms or tentacles reaching out to her...
And certainly. Not. Dessert.

***

I could be exercising instead of sitting here, she thought. No one would be in the gym; no one would look at her. The team mantra of "everybody's work matters; everybody's work affects the bottom line" fell into the same category of bullshit as "one size fits all" and "we guarantee results*; *results shown not typical" and, if she were being honest, "I could be exercising."

She answered phones based on scripts. Averaging under a specific time.

Digging her elbows into her sides, squeezing thighs so fat she had to sit like a man, she tried to take up less space. She clutched her notebook, estimating her budget for the rest of the month after the car repair, potential blood test bill, and missing a day of work.

If she stuck to iceberg lettuce, if salads were on sale... How much sugar *was* in the off-brand meal replacement shake? She'd read an article explaining macros and how they affected digestion and how improperly calculated macros could undo dieting efforts.

Her stomach growled. She glanced around; had anyone heard? A hundred-thousand teeth and snapping cephalopod beaks twirled and spun in her belly, hungry for more than salad. She hunched, trying not to grimace, trying not to move in case she touched someone who'd think *That fucking fat chick is taking up too much space.*

"Do you have a question...?"

She hated the way Jennalise said her name. Her stomach's gnawing made her think, *I could just eat her face.* Slouching to squash her stomach so it didn't feel so hungry, so angry, hoping to be less intrusive, she said, "Sorry. Muscle cramp."

Jennalise's glare suggested she should have muscle cramps at a time that wouldn't interrupt an important team meeting.

She wished she could consume herself, like a black hole, contracting small enough to not interrupt an important team meeting. To not interrupt *anything*.

★★★

After a month of counting calories, reducing sugar, and parking as far away from her work as possible, she decided to go shopping. If she'd made progress, she could buy a new piece of clothing. If she'd failed, she deserved the suffering and needed to be reminded of her goals.

A dress size, a dress size! My life savings for a dress size! Not that she had any savings to offer. Anything left from her squire-level pay of collecting manure through phone conversations went toward the minimum payments of her student loans. Dreams of making the world a better place through communications still needed to be paid for, regardless of being fulfilled or not.

Produce was pricier than pasta; "healthy" labels drew hefty prices even in off brands. Pre-made meals that magically met all macro requirements were not cheap. But if she could just find the right alchemical formula for fat combustion, it would all be worth it.

Just one dress size!

But she found the unicorn: a sweater wrap-dress, one size down, suitable for work. And leggings to match!

For a moment, she felt beautiful.

★★★

She strode into work—a conquering warrior princess *in a dress!* Adorning her headset crown, she could ignore the protesting whale song of springs from her ergonomic throne of pain.

For a moment, she felt powerful.

Jennalise tapped her on her shoulder, summoning her to her office with a sneer. "We need to chat about company dress code."

At least Jennalise had non-ergonomic chairs for her to deflate into.

"What do you mean?"

"What you're wearing is inappropriate."

She closed her eyes. Pictured her manager. Opened them again. Something swirling, dark, and strong manipulated her mouth with boneless arms or tentacles. "You wore an outfit just like this on Monday."

Jennalise narrowed her eyes. "The company policy is clear on leggings and tights not being see-through if you're wearing a skirt that short. That material is stretching enough where I can see your legs. Perhaps you need a larger size."

Burning bile whirling with chalky protein shake bound her tongue. *A larger size?*

"I'll let you stay today. If we have this discussion again, you're going home for the day with no pay. We have clients who tour the facility. They don't want to see... *that*."

She would not cry. She would not cry. *Shewouldnotcry.*

Pressure headache halos spun a wave of dizziness that made her clutch the sides of the chair. Shadow fish in murky water flowed over Jennalise's face, drowning her, pulling her into a liquid pit, a hungry stomach of acid and tangling, sucking tentacle arms—

"You can leave now. You don't want your call numbers to fall too low."

Shewouldnotcry!

The imaginary monsters inside carried her to her ergonomic jail on invisible arms and tentacles, swimming on black-hole waves. The office chair squealed space-whale songs of protest, no matter how gently she tried to sit.

"What's her beef this time?" asked Lettie, her cubemate inside the prison-grey fabric walls.

She shrugged. A verbal confession might let loose the oceans raging behind her eyes.

"Don't let her get to you. Numbers are down and she's probably pissed that dress looks better on you."

Kindness was suspect—a way to open the door for a knife to the gut. That was the lesson she'd learned in school, reinforced regularly if she dared go dancing, smile at a stranger—by accident or on request—sit at a coffee shop in a manner someone thought was too inviting, or even just speak.

Narrowing eyes, she studied her cubemate's back. Lettie's shapeless beige trousers and men's shirts had few enough Xs to be hung in "women's" and "men's" sections that needed no modifiers or special stores or higher prices. She wore no makeup. She wasn't *pretty.* But she was thin.

Suspect.

There were more fat jokes than ugly jokes for a reason.

The starving beast in her belly gnawed and growled its discontent; her headpiece howled and hissed malicious murmurs. Response scripts summoned her through logic labyrinths leading to neither Minotaur nor epiphany, but rather a numb asphodel solace.

Agonized space-whale screams narrated a chair-bound anti-Odyssey—but without any Metamorphoses.

Fat women weren't heroes or princesses; she didn't belong in fantasy any more than she belonged in real life.

***

Properly opaque tights sagged elephant wrinkles at her ankles. Her dress hung past her knees.

The mirror lied—how did one look fatter when one's

clothes were too big?

The scale lied—clothes bought two months ago would cling to such a mass.

Jennalise was honest—but *kind.*

"Ill-fitting clothes are unprofessional. I should send you home with the client coming, but three people called out and our numbers are shit. Make sure you tuck your legs under the desk…"

The chair still squealed its truth; the wheels bored grooves into the plastic mat and rug below. Her stomach's serrated songs still spoke in starvation pangs. Tickling dark tentacles—suckers only on the end—told lies about reality that her eyes still saw and her fingers still felt.

She flicked her wrist every few minutes to see her imaginary cephalopod friends flip from her nails. She folded her hands to feel their touch—inquisitive and unrepulsed.

Something is very wrong with me.

Well yes. You're fat. No one spoke, but that voice was as familiar as…anyone. Everyone. *We just worry about your health, honey. Have you tried…*

Everything. I've fucking tried everything.

Her fingernails dug crescent moons into fleshy palms to quell…tears? Screams? To keep from stealing the fucking M&Ms Lettie always put out between them because she wasn't on a fucking diet and didn't fucking care and probably fucking wanted her cubemate to stay fat so no one noticed how chubby and ugly Lettie was herself?

"Did you get henna somewhere? Or did you draw that just now?"

A piercing ergonomic yelp announced her jump at Lettie's voice.

"Looks cool." Lettie's nod directed attention back to her hands.

Smudged ball-point black ink tentacles coiled and

spiraled down each finger. The pen—

Splat-squirt! "Shit!"

"Shit, yeah. Here." Lettie thrust tissues onto her lap, catching blots of ink that bled from a broken nib. "You should probably go wash up."

Tentacle-bedecked fingers dropped tissue and pen into the trash bin. Space-whales squealed release as she stood. Bathroom-bound footfalls shook cheap cubical walls, trembling push-pin pocked photos and curled motivational posters in her wake.

Her cleaning efforts were as effective as fad diets.

"Jesus Christ. I *told* you the suits were coming today!" Jennalise, perfectly professional-colored lipstick at the ready, stopped at the sink beside her.

I will not cry. I will not cry. Iwillnotcry!

Jennalise sighed and shifted weight to one proper-sized, proper-curved hip hoisted on a non-load-bearing high heel. Her tone was *kind.* "Look, we're all stressed. I understand that. And I know you're *trying.* I get that. Perhaps if you just picked clothes that were more flattering for your size, you'd feel better and that would keep you on track with your diet and work and everything."

Hands on unsympathetic porcelain, eyes on inky fingers smearing, marring pristine whiteness, she clamped her mouth shut lest an ocean pour out, fill the bathroom, drown everything.

"I hear seltzer water gets out stains like that. For now, just dry up and get to your desk so we can get the call numbers under control. I'll see if we can keep the tour from going down your row."

Nod. She could manage a nod. She managed a nod.

Professional-colored lipstick perfectly applied, Jennalise left the bathroom.

Cold water from a cold sink didn't clean her hands.

Paper towels didn't absorb or absolve. Rinsing only smudged stinging ink and mascara into tentacles of darkness around her eyes. Each blink wriggled a wave of "hello" from friends that weren't real.

I can't work. Something's very wrong with me.

Black ink tasted bitter as she poked her throat until she gagged. Burning bile sparsely coated her tongue, blending with chalky vanilla breakfast shake.

She couldn't even do Bulimia right.

But she choked a convincing cascade of dry heaves when she heard the bathroom door open. Wiping stringy spittle, she staggered from a stall.

Lettie stepped backward. "You look like shit. Go home. I'll tell Jennalise you were puking."

Nod. An honest nod.

Inky, stinging tentacles danced in the corners of her vision as she drove to her doctor's office.

"We don't have anything open today. Do you want to go to the emergency room?"

No. She'd take an appointment tomorrow. She'd call in sick. She was the only one who questioned whether she should even be driving with the world swimming in dark oceans.

She hadn't any other choice.

***

309.7

309.7

309.7

It was even .2 lighter than the scale at home. Not nearly enough.

"Isn't it odd that I've gone down two dress sizes and I'm the same weight?"

Her doctor didn't look up from the clipboard. "Clothing companies don't have universal sizing. Some women find as much as four sizes difference between brands."

"It's the same fucking dress I bought two months ago that is now too big for me!"

Sharp doctor eyes didn't like swearing. "Clothes stretch. The numbers are right here. I can give you some antibiotics, but it's more likely a virus. There's a flu going around. Drink plenty of water…"

She knew how to deal with a flu. She didn't know how to deal with tentacles—hallucinations. Fever dreams? The nurse had taken her temperature…what had it been?

"…are you eating enough?" The doctor's question made no sense.

"What?"

"Are you eating enough? Sometimes cutting calories too sharply can make you lightheaded and keep you from actually losing weight."

Squirming pressure wound up from her growling black-hole belly and writhed from her throat to her mouth. "Jesus. Fuck. I can't even!"

She let her footfalls shake the scale, tremble the blood pressure cuffs; the privacy curtain *whooshed* in her wake. Octopi could squeeze their entire mass through holes a quarter of their size. She octopus-flowed between nurses and carts, uncomfortable chairs and perturbed patients until she got to her car.

She collapsed, boneless and blobby, in the seat until the inky, angry swirls in her vision cleared enough to drive to work. Half a day was half more pay than she'd planned, and a fraction less catastrophe come the end of the month.

The tortured whale within her office chair squealed no softer, though the arms dug less deeply into her flesh.

Jennalise was not in. That was good, at least. "Good" as defined by the depressing, maddening, cubicle labyrinth that penned her in. Fat minotaur monstress that she was.

She returned to her car to find a flat tire. Frustrated tears flowed freely. *Fuck. Fuck. Fucking fuck.*

"Hey, what's wrong?" Mark from sales pressed a hand on her back.

She jumped at his touch—*a touch.* How fucked was her makeup? Had she even worn makeup? How shitty, pathetic, disgusting, did she look?

"Looks like you got a flat?"

"Umn-hmn," bubbled through pathetic snot.

"Got a spare in the back?"

"Um...Umn-hmn."

"Pop the trunk?"

Think. Deliberate. Keyfob. Click. *Pop.*

Mark stared at her for she didn't know how long; time stopped being countable.

Why is he staring? Did he just smile? Is he secretly laughing at me? She forced her mouth into a smile back. Women should always smile. *How much of a mess is my trunk? What even is in my trunk?*

Mark tossed his suit coat over the edge of her trunk and rolled up his sleeves. He had muscles that came from working out.

He was already twisting bolts with the tire iron before she thought to stammer, "Th-thank you."

"It's no problem."

"S-sorry. My dad taught me...ages ago...Really, thank you, I'm sorry."

"Really, it's no problem."

"Thank you...and yeah, sorry."

"You apologize a lot."

"Sorry...I-uh, sorry." *Sorry I'm a dumbass. Sorry I exist. Sorry to affect your existence.*

Perhaps his laugh was meant to be kind...He was helping; she should think him kind.

"It's kinda cute," he said. "The apologizing."

Cute? Someone called her cute! Someone who worked out and rolled up sleeves to change her tire called her cute. Oceans and octopi swam warning circles in her stomach.

Kind is suspect.

Men who worked out did not call women like *her* cute.

Mark spoke; only one word registered: "…donut…"

She flinched.

"Where do you live? You don't want to drive more than fifty miles on a donut."

Her mind spun like bald tires on ice. *I don't remember when I last had a donut. He asked where I live. He called me cute. Kind is suspect.* Her mouth managed, "Sorry, I don't live far. And thank you."

After tossing in the tire and iron, he retrieved his coat and slammed the trunk. Then he leaned on the open driver's door like it was his.

"Do you have a regular tire guy or car guy?"

"Um…" She shook her head.

Could she fit through her open, leaned-on door? Like an escaping octopus? Unable to move, she sucked in her churning gut. Even in uncharted territory, she knew she should take up less space.

"Since you don't live far, maybe I could come over to your place and put on the new tire?"

Dark tendrils wriggled on the edges of her vision once again. *Something is wrong. Something is wrong with* me… Blinking didn't clear her eyes. Swallowing didn't calm the hungry, wary, beasts in her belly.

She didn't want a suspicious man to know her address. That's how awful things happened to women. She shook her head. "Sorry…but thank you, really."

He still leaned on her door. "We could meet for coffee tomorrow. I don't live far either, and there's that Starbucks by the highway. I'm pretty much free for the day."

Free for the day tomorrow? Was it already Friday? Where had her week gone?

Where had her *life* gone?

He *still* leaned on her door. Her answer was the toll, the price of her escape. *Is this a date?* He'd called her cute. He'd been kind. He was blocking her escape.

Kindness is suspect.

She wanted just to leave. "I...sure."

"Great! How about two o'clock? That should give you enough time to get a new tire."

She pressed her hand to her belly harder, pulling it in, holding in the frenzy fighting to escape, to consume the potential threat. "S-sure..." she said. It sounded like "S-sorry," an apology to the tummy monsters.

***

She stayed up all night researching tires so she wouldn't look stupid. If he *did* ask to see her again, it would be because he wanted to see her again and not because she'd stupidly bought the wrong tire.

She spent all morning making sure with makeup that he wouldn't know she'd stayed up all night.

He gave her a pumpkin spice latte when she arrived. He hadn't asked what she wanted.

"Th-thank you." Whole milk, so much sugar. How many sit-ups, push-ups, burpees, and miles would she need to fight the consequences of this unwanted gift?

She had a specific order, programmed into her phone and sent as she left for work, so she didn't have to deal with *those looks* when she asked for skim milk, sugar-free, extra espresso to up her metabolism and lower the amount of high-carb milk. She hated *those looks,* those corporate-trained smiles that didn't need words to say, "That's right, fatso. You know better than to suck down even more sugar and fat."

Sipping lightly, she felt another set of *looks* as she sat on the chair that didn't fit her ass, trying to hide her stomach beneath the table lip. "That's right, fatso. That's how you got that gut, drinking all that sugar and fat."

Mark's ass fit in the chair, and there was space between the table and his stomach. His "I did a good thing" smile prompted her to sip again, to stammer again, "Th-thank you. It's good," despite the fact she felt she ought to puke because *so many calories.*

There was a reason bulimia was a "mental illness"; throwing up on purpose didn't work for everyone. She knew it was wrong, but still wished for an actual eating disorder. Insurance was more likely to help with "mental illness" than being fat.

Nothing was worse than being fat.

With coffee drunk, they moved to the tire changing portion of their "date." She paid attention, noting how her trunk elegantly hid a donut tire, a jack, and a tire iron just beneath a false floor panel that reminded her of the "stomach slimming panels" in her specially made jeans, skirts, and trousers.

Her car did a better job concealing extra weight than her clothing.

She leaned on her own car door as he closed the trunk.

"Thank you again." She didn't stutter. *Good start.* She'd made a plan. "I was going to buy *you* coffee to thank you, but you beat me to it." She pulled out a gift card and offered it. "So, next time you go, coffee on me."

He held out his hands and shook his head. "No, no. Don't worry about it. Though…"

The space of his pause strained the breath she was holding.

"You could join me for lunch, or even dinner,

sometime."

He wants to see me again!

Her stomach rumbled, unsated by sumptuous latte sugar and fat. She adjusted her posture—tuck the butt, suck in the gut...

Do I always put my hand on my stomach when I'm nervous? Does it hide how much it sticks out?

Mark looked at her, head tilted like a dog. "Sooo...?"

"Uh-um, yeah. S-sure."

His smile grew—at her answer or returned stammer? "Great. How about next weekend?"

"S-sure!"

How would she get through a week of work? How did one act at work when waiting for a date? *Is this really a date?* Until that moment, she hadn't known how much she wanted it to be a date.

"So, see you Monday?"

"Yeah, Monday." She smiled, thankful he left first. Her body had frozen in place—butt tucked, gut sucked lest she shatter the illusion of being someone that somebody wanted to date.

***

On Monday, Mark said nothing different, did nothing different. She wondered if he'd forgotten, if he *regretted...*

Jennalise was still out. *Thank goodness.* Another "talking to" would have reduced her to useless blubber and tears.

On Tuesday, she reminded herself there was probably some stupid workplace rule that prohibited dating.

On Wednesday, she talked herself out of checking the employee handbook regarding dating prohibition. Jennalise was back; the last thing she wanted was for *her* to ask what rule she was looking up.

On Thursday, her trousers gapped at the waist and she

had to fold a pleat in the back to buckle her belt. When she came back from lunch, before she could sit, before her chair screamed its torture, Lettie stood, grabbed her arm, and stood close—*intimately* behind her.

She froze.

"Honey, your pants' gap is hanging in the back. Your panties are showing!"

How long? Who saw? Everyone, everyone *must have seen.*

"Come with me." Lettie strategically placed herself, leading her to the ladies' room sanctuary from behind. The bathroom's morgue chill matched how she stood corpse-doll still while Lettie assured, "Probably no one saw. Must've just happened. We can fix this easy…"

She was numb to her cubemate's adjusting, refolding, and tucking.

"If you do this closer to the side, you can hold it for now. I'm sure I have a safety pin at the desk, but this should hold for us to walk back."

"Th-thank you."

"My mom lost a bunch of weight on chemo. I learned to help her watch out for wardrobe malfunctions." The question on the end of Lettie's voice invited confession.

She had nothing to share; she could offer no story in payment for kindness. It occurred to her that she had hardly thought about her imaginary cephalopod friends, though they had not left the corners of her vision, hadn't stopped peeking from under her nails, and hadn't stopped their incessant, hungry stomach chewing. "Th-thank you."

With a hard swallow, she stared at the bowl of M&Ms—inky tentacles danced in the dark crevices created between rounded edges of candy-bright tablets.

If she did have cancer, would the doctor still say, "Well if you just lost some weight…"?

Or might cancer be the cure…What kind of monster wished for cancer just to lose weight?

"Oh yeah, the pin." Lettie sat—*her* ergonomic office chair did not whale-scream in protest—and fished in her drawer.

"Th-thank you."

"If this were a fairy tale, you'd owe me a favor."

Her eyes opened so wide, her mouth could not work.

"I'm joking; don't worry. You said 'thank you' three times…That's like magic in fairy tales…three times…Never mind." Lettie looked at the candy bowl.

Does she see what I see in the shadows, the shadows in that bowl and wherever I look?

"I used to read fairy tales." There, she'd made a confession.

Lettie looked up.

There had been a time when hopeful light had danced in *her* eyes, as it did in Lettie's. When she hadn't given up in finding a friend—a real friend, not one who pretended long enough to laugh at the hope dying in her eyes when she learned they were only pretending. When she learned they only wanted her test answers. When she learned they thought she was an easy lay—desperate because no one *really* wanted sex with a fat chick.

"Why did you stop? Reading fairy tales?" Lettie asked.

"I just did." She turned back to her work before she saw the light die in Lettie's eyes.

At least she wasn't the kind of monster who laughed.

On Friday, as she left work in different trousers but still Lettie's safety pin, she couldn't get to the car fast enough. An ocean of tears thrashed behind her eyes, and an army of octopi and squid and even cuttlefish pounded her stomach with their arms and tentacles. Mark had passed her and not even said a word.

But there was an envelope under her windshield wiper. Inside was an address and a time and a smiley face and Mark's name.

Leaning on the car, she shook free the sea in her head and wiped away released tears. The cephalopods did not share her relief; they were still wary. And so very hungry.

***

The sharp taste of blood, the soft tear of flesh—those memories overshadowed and blurred every other moment of the night.

There had been a nice restaurant. He'd ordered food for her. More than a salad...

Blood didn't taste like copper as books described. It was salty and rich like ocean and sand, but warmer in temperature and spice.

She had wanted dessert—she *always* wanted dessert—but she didn't want dessert. He'd said something about how she *must* want dessert. She'd sent back more than half her food *saying* she wasn't hungry. Had he been upset she hadn't eaten his gift?

The muscled flesh of a man's lips tore like raw chicken breast; the blood taste was more like beef.

It would be easier when she was thinner. A man wouldn't say she *ought* to appreciate his gifts. A man wouldn't say she was *lucky* to get his affections. A man wouldn't say she should *let* him kiss her, *let* him lift her dress—a new dress she couldn't afford but felt she needed to look like someone who'd *be* on a date—because how many men even wanted to touch her?

Inside her belly, her imaginary monster friends fought for that tiny scrap of meat.

Had she really bitten?

Bitten *off* his lip?

Had she really chewed?

Had she swallowed?

The taste throbbed on her tongue, the texture against her teeth, as she realized she was in her parking spot outside her apartment and had no recollection of getting in her car, driving away. She flexed her fingers on the gearshift she *must* have manipulated; it felt like alien equipment.

Invading lips, a "hug" that trapped her against her car, invading fingers. She'd craved touch, not violation. Like something wild, she'd bitten to make it stop.

Bitten and chewed and swallowed. Like something monstrous.

Licking her teeth, exploring the lingering flavor, she thought things that sickened her more than the chunk of invading lip that may or may not be swimming in her stomach or consumed by imaginary beasts that lived there and loved her unconditionally.

Someone thought I was worth...doing that *to.* Who would think such a thing? *Me. I would.* Unlike that night, that "date," she clearly remembered sitting through sexual harassment meetings and thinking *I am too fat to even get sexually harassed.*

She leaned on her steering wheel. *I should've just let him...*

The roiling tentacles in her tummy stabbed angry cramps at such a thought. She found strength to get out of her car and get to her apartment before she puked on her overpriced—but another size smaller!—dress. When she made it to her bathroom, she only dry heaved.

Her body, or her beasts, were not giving up the scant portion she'd consumed.

***

Mark was not at work all week.

She wondered if he was all right. She wondered how long it took him to stop bleeding. She wondered if he'd need surgery to replace the lip chunk she'd since shat out and if the sales department had better insurance than the customer servants chained to telephone headsets.

She'd gotten better about pinning her trousers and skirts so they wouldn't fall down—and ignoring her cube mate's growing looks of concern.

She's probably jealous I'm getting thinner and she isn't. Maybe if she didn't keep fucking candy on the desk all the time, she'd get thinner too...

"Get thinner." The scale still lied. Her clothing fit differently, but her weight hadn't changed. Her footsteps still thundered when she walked; her chair still whale-squealed its protest.

Time passed in metered out vegetables, baked chicken breasts, protein shakes (with low carb counts), lots of lemon water, and unsweetened green tea and coffee. Time passed with an ignored student loan, a credit card she couldn't make a minimum payment on, and a blood test with "everything normal" readings that only validated its lack of necessity to her insurance. Rent she managed, along with her specific grocery list, but her car payment was a week late.

She thought she saw Mark back at work, but she avoided looking too closely. The dark tentacles that danced around her vision's edge had grown. She welcomed them; it was easier than worrying about seeing the eye doctor outside of her annual insurance allowance.

Jennalise called her into her office.

Her stomach full of angry tentacles and arms churned. *What now?* She crossed her legs at the ankles; someday, someday she could almost see, she'd be able to do that confident knee cross thin and powerful women could do.

From the way she sat in her manager's chair, Jennalise was crossing her legs like *that*. "A team member has brought up a sexual harassment complaint against you."

"*What?*" She nearly stood.

Jennalise's finger pointed, a magical force freezing her to the false-comfort chair.

Does a pointy painted finger taste like intrusive lips?

Jennalise continued, "Human Resources is investigating it now. You'll get a formal letter from them shortly. But between that, your regular flouting of dress code..." Her eyes narrowed and scanned up and down.

I. Will. Not. Squirm. She clenched her teeth but still shifted her crossed ankles.

"...and all your absences lately, it's not looking good for you."

She sucked and snorted breaths through her nose like a bull. "I. Did not—"

Pointing finger. Perfectly manicured. Polish probably tasted bad. The finger was so thin, how much of a bite would it take? Dark tentacles drew her focus to the target; her stomach churned and growled.

If Jennalise heard the hunger or saw movement beneath the pinned waistband of the grey, ankle-length skirt that fell in too many folds, she didn't respond. Instead, she said, "I can't talk about the sexual harassment issue with you until human resources has investigated."

Acid seeking something to digest burned up her throat, threatening to eat her if she didn't feed the dry-chomping teeth in her belly.

With a *kind* smile, Jennalise continued, "I just wanted to give you a heads up. So you're not blindsided by anything on your annual review."

If she opened her mouth, the tentacles and arms following the acid and choking her would burst forth and pull Jennalise toward the unnatural hunger. That would also look bad on her annual review. And how many burpees would she have to do this weekend to burn off the managerial calories?

Jennalise shuffled papers on her desk, a dismissal.

If she stood, would the beasts burst from her belly like a horror-movie monster? When had she started to think of *them* as real?

"You should get back to the phones. Your times aren't that great either, you know."

Biting her tongue, she compared the taste of her own blood to Mark's. Hers tasted more bitter, but it sated or distracted her—*and them*—so she could stand and leave.

Frightened of herself, of the thoughts floating in her mind and the darkness swimming in her vision, she sacrificed a little extra cash to add steak to her salad in hopes of appeasing...*herself.*

***

312.4

How? The fuck?

"You've gained some weight since your last visit," her doctor said. "I thought you were working on losing."

"I am. Look at me."

"Perhaps we should try an appointment with our weight center..." She started scribbling the referral.

"I tried that two years ago and insurance won't cover it. *Look* at me."

"I am looking, and I'm seeing a big problem—"

"You're *looking* at the computer screen. Look at *me*. Do I *look* like I weigh three-hundred and twelve fucking pounds?"

Her doctor looked at her with Jennalise's narrow, judging eyes. At least she didn't point a finger, but all *she* saw was a contentious fat bitch. "Good clothing can hide your weight, and you can't see how fat fills in between your organs—"

"I bought these pants and shirt at Walmart a year ago. And this is how they fit now!" She held out the safety-pinned fold at the waist. "Something else is wrong if I'm getting smaller and my weight is going up."

The beasts inside her, the beasts she'd stopped calling imaginary, were filling in space and writhing between her organs. At the moment, they squeezed her lungs, making it painful to breathe. Her heart beat double time, constricted by the hug of cephalopod limbs.

"Your bloodwork is normal. Perhaps today's gain is water weight. Watch your salt and make sure you drink enough. I'm scheduling a follow-up for another three months, and if you still feel something else is wrong, we can explore other options."

A fresh appointment sheet ended the conversation. Slid across the table, it didn't even put a body part within biting distance.

***

She received no sexual harassment notice from Human Resources. Not wanting to ask Jennalise, she chose not to think about it. When she saw a silhouette or shadow resembling Mark, she refused to even look.

Ignoring medical copays and yet another month of student loans, she splurged on a dress for the office holiday party. It was the largest size from the normal-sized women's section at Nordstrom's. It was gold and beautiful and *it fit*.

Jennalise wore the exact same dress to the party. She didn't point or poke a finger, but the knives in her eyes were tangible.

She couldn't tell if it were by chance or on purpose that Jennalise entered the bathroom as she was washing her hands, ready to leave.

With a *kind* smile, Jennalise said, "You know, that color and cut really don't flatter your body size. Clothes more suited to your shape would make you feel better when you dress up. Black is slenderizing, and it'd match your shoes."

All she owned for fancy shoes were black Mary Janes with a little heel. She hadn't had money to buy matching shoes.

Having grown large enough to fill her torso and hug every organ, her beasts—her friends—writhed up her throat and out her mouth. They'd taken her hunger and made it theirs. And they hated when people made her want to cry.

Jennalise's eyes widened, but she had no chance to scream. It took less time than she imagined to consume the bitch who fed her ego on others' misery. On *her* misery.

Locking the main bathroom door, she washed Jennalise's bloodstained dress in cold water. Cold water worked better on blood than ink. She grabbed Jennalise's matching gold heels. Standing far enough back from the handicapped sink's mirror, she looked at her entire body and was not disgusted.

Lettie had been right. She looked better in Jennalise's clothes than Jennalise did.

After careful checks, she exited the bathroom, grabbed her coat, left the office. Quickly. She had less invisibility in her smaller size. At least her too-big black coat covered the glimmering gold dress.

"Hey, you fat cunt!" There was a fresh lisp to the familiar voice.

The words sucked her confidence like the last sip of coffee on a Monday. And reawoke the beasts from semi-sated sleep. She spun; Jennalise's heel betrayed her. Sharp pain twisted her ankle as she fell with a yelp.

Of course Mark laughed. Of course he had friends with him. Their alcoholic amusement dulled the night's sharp frost scent.

Parking lot lights reflected off snow piles and the gleam

of scars on Mark's upper lip.

She laughed, kicked off the golden heels, and let ice-cold pavement scrape through the cheap pantyhose that still dug into her groin while sagging at her ankles. She headed toward the farthest parking spot in the lot, swimming in the coat she'd bought to hide her shape, her edges, her curves, her rolls.

"You fucking fat bitch. You think you can laugh at my friend here that you *mutilated*?"

"A guy tries to kiss someone like you, you better fucking appreciate it!"

Still walking, she raised two middle fingers. Tiny tentacles—babies of her beastly friends?—slipped out and hugged her fingers in response. Inside, her stomach rumbled and writhed.

Inside, she was still hungry.

Pounding steps in shiny men's shoes walked, then jogged, behind her.

Hunger overpowered the asphalt's bites on her feet. Memory, not fear, hurtled her to her car, reached a hand to her pocket, clicked the keyfob to open the trunk.

Hands grabbed, finding only a coat that hid a lack of flesh. Like an escaping octopus, she slipped away unhindered.

Flipping open the panel that hid her spare tire, she grabbed the iron. Guided by cephalopod arms—stronger per inch than human ones—she spun and swung. She spun and swung with more limbs than a human. With unexpected alien muscles, she grabbed and twisted and crushed.

And consumed.

Office mates left the party; none looked toward the far corner of the parking lot.

When hunger no longer gnawed, when the cold

pavement bit and chewed harder than her befriended beasts, she stuffed the tire iron and the leftovers into her trunk. Blood stained the dress and her face and skin yet again. Dirty snow provided enough cold water to wash it away.

She collected her too-big, boring black coat and wrapped herself in its waves.

Cephalopods were masters of disguise, and she needed to hide.

While she no longer embodied the greatest sin of being a woman and fat, she was still carnal sin.

She was a woman and unafraid.

EATING SINS FOR FUN AND PROFIT

Societies crave sin-eaters. They want someone to face the madness for them.—Adam Stemple

Don't take medicine,
        they say.
Wander the woods, sit by a pond—
        hike a mountain, stare at a lake.
That's what the greats *did.*
Whitman, Coleridge, Hemingway—
        even Poe
would walk shadowed streets for inspiration,
        to face the demons.
Poe found death delirious in those streets,
self-medicated with laudanum and alcohol.
What further dreams could have been penned
        with proper therapist, different prescription?
If Plath had not needed to scream into the void of her oven?
If Sanmao had not sought comfort in silk stockings' final swing?

But all you artists, poets, musicians, creators
        drink, drug yourself, entertain orgies—
All part of the process.
Eccentric, not crazy. Creative brains work differently—
        another way to say neuroatypical.
How else could one put ink to paper, paint to canvas,
mouth to microphone,

and bleed the things
others dare not say, not think, not do?
Exorcise lust, pain, fear of death,
        lust for death,
                and all that's taboo.
Catharsis without confessional,
        bypassing purgatory via vicarious vivisection
of disfigured muses, naked and shivering—
        sacrificed on the audience's behalf.

We're all mad here.
We paint our Cheshire smiles
        while studying the mirror's play of light on tears,
        the musical strains of choking screams,
        the characterization of fear—
                or more frightening, love.
Spin immoralities, debaucheries, inequities into words and
notes and pictographs of gold,
        offered in exchange for new life,
only to have our names stolen.
Demons, goblins, fey unnamed and neutered,
        we suffer indigestion from your sins.

AT LEAST THE CHICKENS
ARE ALL RIGHT

AT LEAST THE CHICKENS ARE ALL RIGHT

Chickens are way cooler than most people think. First of all, they're the closest thing we have to actual dinosaurs —which I always think more people know than actually do. But chickens are also smarter than most people think. You can train them to do tricks...and like pretty much any animal, they train their humans to care for them.

While there are diseases and mites that affect chickens, there's a lot of stuff they're immune to. So besides laying eggs and generally being cute, chickens are good for barns because they eat insects and bugs that carry infections to other animals, including humans.

Chickens are also omnivores. They will kill and eat small animals, like rodents, birds, or snakes that threaten their eggs or their coop. It was the dead things that stayed dead that clued me in to the relationship between chickens and surviving an apocalypse.

The dead things *not* staying dead started up a couple of weeks ago. Day-Day, the barn cat, brought a chipmunk into the office. A chipmunk that shoulda been dead but, after ten minutes and having its back half eaten, started running around, trailing its intestines and dropping squirming worms. It traumatized Lenore, one of the stable owners and the mom of our riding instructor and horse trainer, Macy (aka Stable Mom's Mom, aka Stable Gramma). No one else was around, and no one started talking about it until after Chuck, Macy's Dad, (aka Stable Grumpy Grandpa) set another dead-but-not-dead chipmunk on fire.

'Course, we were already under quarantine for lessons because someone reported a rabid skunk in the neighborhood. I got around the quarantine and could volunteer because I'd gotten a rabies shot when a bat got into my family's house last fall. Macy's family and the horse's actual owners (we boarded six horses at the stable) were also allowed access.

When Day-Day ended up dead-but-not-dead, though, I started wondering if it was really rabies that the skunk had.

I hate to use the term "undead," because I've seen plenty of monster movies, and the animals weren't like zombies or vampires. They basically acted like they *did* have rabies—only, if you looked at their bodies, they were definitely dead. At least Day-Day was, for sure. I saw her before…well…I couldn't watch when Chuck took out the heavy shovel and kerosene, but I heard.

I heard about the chipmunks from Gail, who was horse-mommy to Candy, a gorgeous paint who boarded here. She was there when Day-Day came in on three legs, blood smeared over half her side, looking like she'd gotten hit by a car. Wriggling strings—like maggot earthworms—hung from her hip and wounds. She'd been carrying something. I didn't get close enough to see if her prey was also dead-but-not-dead. She'd dropped it and started meowing her proud, "Look what I caught" call—like she always did when she brought us gifts. Chuck, who'd been cleaning stalls, cussed (which he tried not to do around us younger kids) and grabbed the heavy shovel. That's when Gail grabbed me and pulled me into Candy's stall. I didn't fight her; I'd just frozen in the middle of the hall.

Gail pulled me close to Candy and wrapped us in a hug that muffled the sounds. I won't ever forget the hissing yowls and the *clang-crunch* of the shovel. Then the *scrape-scrape*. I was still plastered against Candy, Gail's arm around me, when the smell of kerosene, burning meat, and hair overpowered the pleasant smell of warm horse, citronella, and sweet grain.

I didn't say anything to my mom when she picked me up. She mouthed an "I'm sorry" as she tapped her Bluetooth headset and gave a series of "Uh-huh...Yes... Yes...No, we need to adjust that procedure for the client" responses. That was fine; I didn't *want* to talk about what had happened. A quiz on Friday was my excuse for being quiet and not hungry at dinner. Both my parents asked if they could help. I told them it was American history, knowing that was both of their worst topics, and promised them I was getting help. I sometimes wonder if "good parent" guilt is a thing like survivor's guilt; all my friends complain about their parents. Mine? Let's just say they've put up with a lot between me and my sister and they *still* take time off from work when the school does something stupid, like puts the wrong gender and my deadname on formal paperwork.

I worked at the barn Monday through Thursday unless I had a doctor or psych appointment. Or was sick or had massive homework piles. When I got out of school the next day, I did debate which bus to get on: the one that'd take me home to study, or the one to the barn.

I chose the barn. As sick as I felt climbing the stairs, I really wanted to know what was going on.

When I got to the barn, Macy said they were burying Day-Day's ashes that afternoon. I joined the circle of her family and a few boarders for the beginning, then just had to go. I felt bad, but the few who noticed me leaving gave me understanding looks.

I went to clean the chicken coop. It's a gross job, but it's hard to let your mind wander between the cleaning and watching whatever weird antics the chickens are up to.

Normally, if I get done early, I pull out my sketch pad and draw them like the little dinosaurs they are.

The coop is a converted stall that has plenty of space for them to roam inside or outside but lets us easily lock them inside at night. You can look from the stall-turned-coop into the stable's main hall. Across the way is Candy's stall.

Candy was stomping around and letting out little squeals. "It's okay, Candy," I called to her without looking, because the first challenge of coop cleaning is getting *into* the coop without the chickens escaping. I felt bad; horses, like all animals, know when their humans are upset. And Candy had been so good yesterday, letting Gail and me snuggle her rather than freaking out herself when something scary was happening.

But I didn't want to think about yesterday.

I slipped into the coop with the wheelbarrow and pitchfork and shut the door behind me without any escapees. Then froze again as I wheeled into the outdoor part.

Miss Kate, Pepperoni, and Murica were squawking, taking turns pecking at a half-gone mouse body. I swallowed hard and edged closer. I didn't want to—but *wanted* to—see if it was dead-but-not-dead.

Dead dead. I let out an exhale that hurt my chest. There wasn't much but skin and a few bones to the carcass. And definitely no movement outside the chickens' efforts.

Then Gail screamed for Macy. I hadn't even heard her come in.

I wanted to go help Gail—especially after yesterday— but I froze once again. I hated myself for being a coward.

The little rooster, Chickaletto, pecked at my ankles and made me jump. Which made him puff his chest and lunge. With a frown, I squatted and managed a soothing voice as I said, "Hey, buddy, it's me. It's Drew. We're cool, remember?" I put down the pitchfork and showed him my open hand, appreciating the distraction from the voices and stomping outside the coop.

Though my fingers shook, the rooster didn't seem to care as he hunkered down in his "You may pet me" stance—wings relaxed, half-squatting, beak up, and eyes half-closed. I rubbed one finger against his comb and over his eyes. After a few minutes, he informed me we were done with a shake of his wings and a dart of his head.

The din outside had quieted. Gail was talking softly to Candy, though I couldn't make out the words. I decided to check the nest boxes, which were closer to the hall, and listen in.

"Everything's going to be all right, Candy. You're gonna be okay…"

I peeked through the slats to see. All the stalls had bars, which kept the horses from being able to stick their heads out (and kept annoying unsupervised children from easily sticking their hands in). Gail was a few steps back from the stall, and I could see why.

Candy was circling and stomping. A froth of black, red, and white foam made a beard around her mouth, which was disturbing enough, but hardly the worst. Along her snout, cheeks, and neck, the skin was cracked and peeling—like when you forget gloves during winter chores, only it was a really hot May. No blood was flowing, but the tears were red and angry. I couldn't see very well because she was throwing her head around, snorting and squealing like she was in pain, which she probably was.

Her eyes, though…They were dark and shriveled in their sockets, with yellow and black pus oozing from them. Dead eyes.

Every so often, she'd get close to the bars, bang her head and squeal, stumbling.

The other stalls were empty. Macy must've had everyone move the other horses. Good idea.

Gail was shaking even more than I was. Sometimes she'd edge close to the bars, but a quick turn and squeal from Candy would make her flinch back. "I'm so sorry, baby! The vet's on his way. He'll make this better…"

If it were my horse, if I had a horse, I'd probably be lying to it, too. Because I honestly didn't think Dr. Mac could make Candy better. My stomach turned, and I felt like I'd puke out the chocolate milk and two slices of pepperoni pizza I'd gotten for lunch at school.

I focused really hard on collecting eggs and piling them on a hay bale outside to be brought in later. I checked the dead mouse every time I passed it. It stayed dead.

I wondered how long it took for the dead things to change. It'd been two weeks since Day-Day had brought in that first chipmunk, and it hadn't been till yesterday evening that anyone'd noticed something wrong with her and had to…kill her. Kill her *again*? Candy had been fine yesterday.

I wondered if I should set the mouse body on fire…but, to be honest, I'm a pretty boring kid. My parents didn't smoke, and I never actually played with matches. I basically sit alone and draw things. I figured I'd do that forever because I hated interacting with people. Then my older sister dragged me out to the barn because she had to "babysit" me one Saturday when both our parents had to work, and I loved it. That was two summers ago. Now she was in college and couldn't come with me as often. But Macy gets me. She always calls me by the right pronouns. Sometimes I'll watch/hang out with her youngest son, Rayce, who's five, while she teaches a lesson. Rayce and I both love dinosaurs, animals, and being covered in dirt, so it's cool. I wondered how he was doing—he'd been at the burial—as I berated myself for being a loser who didn't know how to start a fire, even if it meant preventing the infected-dead-rodent-and-barn-animal apocalypse.

I'd cleaned out most of the coop when I heard the diesel pickup truck rumble and stop in our dirt parking lot. The door opened, heavy boots hit the dirt, the door slammed, and Dr. Mac and Chuck started talking in voices they were struggling to keep quiet. I checked my phone. It'd only been a half an hour. Record time for the vet to show up.

They weren't close enough for me to make out words, but their tone squeezed my lungs so that just breathing hurt.

Macy came down the barn hall. "Dr. Mac needs you to sign some paperwork..."

"I didn't bring c-c-cash or a ch-checkbook with me today..." Gail blubbered.

"It's all right, sweetie, we know you. We'll work something out."

They headed back toward the barn office.

I didn't know what was left of Candy behind her dead eyes, but she didn't seem to like Gail leaving. She squealed, groaned, and started beating at the stall door. Cowardly loser me froze again, holding a pitchfork full of hay and chicken shit over the wheelbarrow.

The chickens looked mildly curious about the ruckus.

Chickaletto let out a low crow that reminded me of the velociraptor noises in the *Jurassic Park* films. Even though I'd heard the sound a hundred times or so, it sent goosebumps over my arms.

The office door shut, and the voices of Chuck and Dr. Mac approached. Twisting my sore arms, I flipped the shit into the wheelbarrow and stepped closer to listen.

"...Yeah. Like the others," Dr. Mac said.

"You think it spread to the other horses?"

"Hard to say. We think the flies might be carrying it.

We'll know for sure when…" He trailed off.

I couldn't see them, but I felt a tenseness in the pit of my stomach in those few seconds of silence, in the soft shift of canvas and leather and jeans.

"Hmm. Sorry, Candy," Chuck said with a crack in his voice I hadn't heard before. "Do what you need to, Mac."

Bang.

The gunshot sound punched me in the gut. I staggered backward, tripping over my boot ties and falling ass-first into the pile of chicken shit and hay I'd raked up.

Th-thud. THUD. The sound of something big stumbling. Falling to the ground.

The pitchfork handle fell into my lap as I slapped one hand over my mouth and the other to my chest because I thought my heart had literally stopped.

The stall door rolled open. Not the one to the coop. Candy's. Did they know I was here? The chickens clucked and crowed and flapped up a storm. Maybe their noise covered my fall.

"Yeah…" came Dr. Mac's voice. It was soft but sounded perfectly clear over the quieting chickens. "It is."

"Shit," said Chuck. "What do we do?" Pause. "Fire in here'll send up the whole barn."

"Mmn." Dr. Mac sighed audibly. "Let's check the other animals first. Text Macy. Tell her not to let anyone in the stall."

"Shit," was all Chuck said back.

Candy's stall door rolled closed. Its metal slide-lock *thunked* louder than I'd ever heard it before. Their footsteps headed toward the other end of the stables.

I picked myself up and did my best to clean off my ass. The clearest thought in my head was how pissed Mom would be if I got chicken shit in her car. Maybe I could borrow a towel to sit on.

Making myself think normal things, I stared at the coop's wooden slats as if I could see through them, across the hall, and into Candy's stall. Up until yesterday, I hadn't seen anything die before, seen it killed.

Dr. Mac shot Candy.

Also in my head, I knew, *I knew,* that she hadn't really been alive. Or if she was, she was in a lot of pain. That she couldn't've been fixed.

Dr. Mac shot Candy.

I'd heard gunshots before, in the distance. The stables were near woods where people hunted. I'd never touched a gun—boring kid, remember? Couldn't even think of a time I'd seen one up close. Not even at Walmart. I didn't frequent the sporting goods section.

Dr. Mac shot candy.

I looked over at the mouse. Still dead. Mostly skin and bones. The chickens kept pecking at it.

Not knowing what else to do and not wanting to leave the chicken coop—my sanctuary—I finished shoveling crap into the wheelbarrow. It didn't take but a minute. I was staring at the wheelbarrow, not ready to push it out to Poop Mountain across the street, when I heard the office door slam and feet come jogging up the hall.

"H-hey, Candy…"

It was Gail. I crept back inside. Candy's stall door rolled open, freezing me in place (a trend in my life right now). I'd unfrozen and taken two more steps before I was shocked still again.

"Fucking God! Fuck! Fu—" Violent puking cut off Gail's last swear.

It was all I could do to not throw up, too.

"I'm sorry…" Gail apologized. "I didn't mean to…but *God!* How do you have all those maggots in your face already? How fucking strong was that gun? There's like nothing but—those *worms…"*

Worms? Like the things on Day-Day? And the chipmunk?

"Ow!" A hard slap rang from the stall. "Stupid fucking fly. Killed you, you bast—*The fuck?* Ew! My God, ew!" Gail ran from the stall, each stride punctuated with another "Ew!"

Holding the pitchfork in one hand, I chased the chickens away from the inside door. I slowly opened it so it didn't squeak, closed it behind me so the chickens wouldn't get out, and crept over to where Candy's stall was still open.

The horse lay on her side, a stained blanket over her neck and face. The opposite wall was splattered with black and red…*bits.* As well as tags of skin and tufts of hair. And long pink-white worms. Longer than maggots, but smaller than earthworms. Some were half-splattered with their intact body squirming, stuck, on the wall. Others curled and crawled between the wall's boards.

Keeping my distance, I reached with the pitchfork to lift the blanket off Candy's face. I only saw motion, squirming, before—

Bang!

From the office.

What! The! Fuck?!

I dropped the blanket and ran back to the coop, barely closing the door without a sound while keeping the chickens inside.

What even…? As I fought the pain of just breathing, Chickaletto ran up and started pecking at my boots.

"Hey! Hey!" I breathed, backing away and dropping the pitchfork.

Another peck yanked one of those worms from my boot.

"Fuck! Fuckfuckfuckfuckfuck!" I scraped backward

several steps and then checked my boots. No more worms. But Blueberry, Machete, Murica, half the flock went at the pitchfork, fighting for the couple of worms that had clung to it. I checked every inch of my feet, ankles, legs, clothes, *everything*. When I felt I was safe, I grabbed the now-clean pitchfork and wheeled the barrow out of the coop and across the street to dump it.

Would the chickens get infected now? If the chickens got infected, that would be my fault.

What did Dr. Mac shoot in the office?

Macy's kids had been here for Day-Day's service. They usually hung out in the office. Had they been in there? And seen…what?

Another barn cat? One of the office rabbits?

I shouldn't have looked in Candy's stall.

Not Gail. I thought of her screaming, running to the office. No way he'd shoot an actual person…No way!

I probably shouldn't have still been in the barn. I don't know where I'd've gone…I still had to wait for one of my parents to pick me up. On autopilot, I put away the wheelbarrow and the pitchfork.

Who—*what*—did Dr. Mac shoot in the office?

Everyone was still in the office when Mom pulled up, so I hopped in the car without saying goodbye. I didn't want answers to the awful questions in my head.

"Hey, sweetie," she said, ruffling my hair, which I normally hated because I was almost fourteen and too old for that. This time, though, her silly touch felt comforting and I found it just a little easier to breathe. "What's wrong? You look bothered."

Shit, what was I going to tell her? I sucked at lying. "The cat died and one of the horses was sick…so it was a tough day." Not a complete lie.

With a frown and creased brow, Mom asked, "Rabies?

Did anything bite you?"

"No. Not rabies." That wasn't a lie. "It was just…hard. Y'know?"

"I'm sorry, kiddo." She one-arm hugged me before putting the car into reverse. "Still, anything I should know about? Are you going to come straight home tomorrow?"

"I dunno. Macy'll probably call if it's something important." Like creepy-ass worms or the barn being burnt down to stop them…

She scrunched her face. "Well, throw all your clothes right in the washer when we get home and take a hot shower…okay?"

Normally, I was annoyed at being told to wash my clothes and take a shower, but this time I couldn't agree more.

***

I spent the next day in a grey haze where I didn't remember anything and managed to be even quieter than usual. Enough that Mrs. Lambert, my science teacher, stopped me on the way out of class and asked me if I was all right or if something was happening in my life. I don't remember what I said, but it was enough to appease her.

I hesitated after the dismissal bell, debating once again which bus to take. Home or the barn?

I didn't remember deciding; I didn't even know what I chose until I recognized the suburbs thinning into the hilly farmland on the way to the stables.

We were about ten minutes from the stop closest to the barn when everyone-on-the-bus's cell phones—maybe eight altogether—screamed that emergency broadcast tone.

"What the fuck?" said one kid; I think his name was Brian.

I didn't say anything. I just stared at the screen.

This is an urgent message from the U.S. Department of Health and Human Services (HHS). The U.S. Centers for Disease Control and Prevention (CDC) has confirmed that individuals in Central and Western Massachusetts have been diagnosed with an unknown parasite transmitted via bug bite.

Public health officials are working together to identify those who might have been bitten by the insect carrying the parasite. They are also working to identify all those who have been in contact with the individuals who have been infected. Authorities will continue to assess the best course of action as they learn more.

At this time, it is unknown how many people have been exposed to the parasite. The first symptoms are asymmetrical welts with raised lines; intense itching and pain; open, bleeding sores with colored discharge; or the appearance of a worm-like parasite on the skin or within an open wound. Based on the information available now, public health authorities have determined that the best course of action is for everyone in the area experiencing these symptoms to report to one of the specialty clinics in the following cities…

My heart hammered. The rest of the information was where the "specialty clinics" were and contact info and an all-caps note about NOT reporting to hospitals. I closed the message and clicked over to my messenger app. My foggy brain hadn't thought to check it before the buses, and I'd had to keep it disabled while in class. A message from Macy said not to come to the barn. *Shit.* I was almost there; what was I supposed to do?

Not coming up with any other ideas, I got off at my usual stop and trudged my usual route. The air felt cold, but it was still May and there were birds singing in the trees. A horsefly buzzed by me and I spazzed out, slapping and hitting and spinning and running till I was sure it was gone and had not bitten me.

"Hey, Drew, what are you doing here?" Macy asked, coming out of the office with a look of concern on her face. "Didn't you get my message?"

"I just got it." I held up my phone. "Didn't see it till I was on the bus."

"I left a message with your mom, too." She frowned, folding her arms. Her eyes were red like she'd been crying, or trying not to.

"What's going on?" I asked. Playing dumb helped way more often than most people realized.

Macy sighed. "A shit-storm. Did you get that emergency message thing on your phone?"

"Yeah, but it was confusing. Bugs?" I swallowed. "Is that what got Day-Day?"

"We don't know. Probably, maybe…Dr. Mac's looking into it…" Her voice trailed off.

With or without a gun? I thought but didn't say.

"Hey, did you get bitten by any bugs lately?" She wore her full-on Worried Mom face now.

I shook my head and pulled out the giant spray can of Deep Woods Off that I always kept in my bag. "I pretty much bathe in this daily."

"Good! Keep bathing in it. Bugs are nasty things. Put another coat on now while we figure out what to do with you…"

I did so, then asked, "Can I go see the chickens?"

"Yeah, go ahead, but stay outside the coop." She pulled out her phone and began texting. Probably looking for someone to drive me home.

I walked along the coop's edge, chatting with the chickens, sticking my fingers through the wire to pet the ones who wanted to be petted. As I walked, I kicked up what, at first, looked like a dead leaf, but stiffer and heavier. I squatted to take a closer look, then recoiled.

It was a chipmunk carcass, but this one looked at least a week or two old. Holey skin and some bones, it was definitely still dead. A flattened, pecked husk. Pursing my lips, I checked the rest of the wire's perimeter and the corners I hadn't done quite that good a job of cleaning yesterday. I found one more very dead mouse carcass and a dead barn sparrow. No worms. I studied each of the chickens. They all looked bright eyed and not-rabid.

My phone rang, making me jump.

"Drew, where are you?" It was Dad.

"At the barn."

"Okay…can you stay late? Or can someone drive you home?"

"Why?" I asked, not liking the panic in Dad's voice.

"Nothing to worry about, really," he said in a voice that meant otherwise. "It's just, your mom got bit by a bug of some sort yesterday or the day before and it's swelling. The hospital sent her to this special clinic and I have to drive her…It's probably nothing, but we just want to be safe. Especially after that weird broadcast message, you know? But, like I said, it's probably nothing. In case we're late, there's leftovers in the fridge…Are you there, Drew?"

"Yeah…Here…" I choked out.

"You all right?"

"Fine. I'll ask Macy for a ride home." I don't know how I managed not to stammer.

"Good, good. I'll keep you posted on things. Love you, kiddo."

"Love you too, Dad. And…and tell Mom I love her."

"Will do. See you later."

I stared at my phone, not hanging up my end even though the screen said Dad had hung up his. My stomach churned icy numbness.

"Was that your parents?" Macy strode toward me and stopped. "What's wrong, Drew?"

I turned slowly to face her. "Mom. Got bit by a bug. And was sent to…one of those…" What had Dad and the message called them?

Macy's face got really pale. We stared at each other for a few moments until a low growl interrupted us.

"Drew, get behind me!" Macy ordered.

I did, looking in the direction of the sound.

Pibly was the black-and-white-and-brown, wire-haired, third-generation mutt that belonged to the closest neighbor a mile down the road. He'd gone missing over this past weekend. Now he stood, growling at us. Half his head was bashed in and his whole side was torn open, revealing his ribs.

Both injuries were teeming with worms.

"Motherfucker," Macy cursed, assuming an alpha posture but backing away, herding me with her. "Chuck's heavy shovel is just inside the doors," she said to me softly. "If we keep backing up, how quick you think you can get it for me?"

"I-I don't know," I said honestly, picturing myself tripping over my feet and falling as the infected dog leapt at Macy and mauled her.

The chickens were all clucking and crowing again,

flapping and hopping around. They weren't running away, though. That seemed odd, against a bigger predator. Macy narrowed her eyes at them, too. She'd raised chickens since she was a kid; I didn't know anyone who knew chickens better than her.

"We're by the coop's gate..." I suggested.

"I'm not letting that thing near my chickens!"

A thought was clawing my brain like a hungry raptor. "Trust me?" squeaked all the way up from my stomach.

Macy screwed her mouth up, looked at me, looked at the wormy dog, then looked at the chickens fluttering and squawking at the gate. "Fuck." She dodged to the side long enough to unhitch the coop door. It swung open. Chickaletto and the hens surged out and onto the dog.

"That is *not* normal chicken behavior!" Grabbing my arm, she darted toward the open barn doors and Chuck's shovel. Next to the shovel was the kerosene tub.

The dog broke through the chicken mob and Macy swung the shovel, hitting it right in the head. It fell and the chickens swarmed the body.

"Did you get any of those worm things on you?" she demanded, checking the bottoms of her feet and pant legs.

I did the same. "No."

Backing away, Macy took the kerosene I'd thought to grab and glared at the birds. "Y'know, guys, I can't burn it with you all on it!"

The chickens were undeterred and continued to feast.

"Chickens are still dinosaurs," I muttered.

"Not gonna argue." She put down the kerosene. As she bent, her shirt rode up her back and I saw an asymmetrical welt just over her jeans' waistband. A thin line of black and red liquid and yellow-white pus dripped from it. Just above her belt, I swore I saw a wriggle—like a worm under her skin.

"M-Macy …?" I started to ask.

"Mommy! Mommy!"

Eyes wide, Macy turned to face the two children running up the hill from the farmhouse she lived in. "What are you two doing here? I told you to stay home with Gramma!"

"Dreeeewwwwwww!" Rayce came running right at me, arms wide. Outside of his mom, I was the only one he chose to hug. He threw his little arms around me before I even registered what he was doing.

"I asked you two a question!" Macy demanded in mom tones.

"We came up because Gramma won't wake up and Keelie's kittens got worms!" Jaylin, Macy's nine-year-old daughter said.

"Worms?" Macy choked on the word.

"Yeah! Worms!" Rayce pulled away from me and held up a handful of wriggling white and pink. He frowned with an "Ow!" and I saw the lines of movement crawling up his chubby little forearm, under his skin.

I backed away, patting my hands under my shirt, and yelped as I felt slimy movement on my back, crawling under my binder. I slapped at the things, trying to brush them off, but I *felt* them still there, going in with pricking bites.

"Fuck, fuck, fuck…" I whispered.

Tears poured down Macy's face as she dropped to one knee. "C'mere, kiddo," she croaked.

"What's wrong, Mommy?" Rayce asked, hesitating.

Jaylin hadn't moved. She was looking at her arms. Panic darkened my vision, so I could only imagine what she was seeing.

I heard a growling crow behind me, like one of the velociraptors from the *Jurassic Park* movies, and turned around. Chickaletto fixed me with a sharp, predatory look.

"H-hey, b-buddy," I stammered to him.

He hopped away from the feasting flock, darting his head between Macy and me. Miss Kate, Murica, and Machete followed him, their eyes bright and hungry.

BETTER HORRORS AND GARDENS

Let me tend my movie monsters,
    garden my gothic ghosts,
    bloom roses of arterial spray.
Let me paint my façade of gore with gorgeous purpose
    over this grotesque house of warped mirrors
    reflecting the illusion of lost control.
Myself and not myself—not really—
More real.
More real than real-mirror lies
    reflecting my made-up clown mask,
hiding horrors inside my skin,
my mind.
Bonafide blood-and-tissue-smeared thighs,
    authentic purple-bloomed bruises
    make certified doctors recoil, turn away.
My own ghost fades in once-loving eyes.
Whispers weave security for actual monsters,
    within their hunting ground of HOA-perfect homes—
all full of decoratively shattered mirrors
    reflecting the illusion of control.

HEART OF
FRANKENSTEIN

HEART OF FRANKENSTEIN

My creator, Victor Frankenstein, promised to make me a mate—an equal to love—in return for my promise that we two would retreat into wilderness far from mankind. He aborted that promise, so I broke mine. Instead, I vowed to unmake him through torment equitable to his transgressions upon me. *That* promise I fulfilled, but not with joy. I then made a new promise: I would surrender to the Arctic's icy prison, righteous judgment of my daemonly wickedness.

And I did for some time.

But Frankenstein's hubris damns me still. What he created was not life, for what is alive must certainly die. I waited, entombed in ice atop the world as Dante's Lucifer was frozen deep below Hell, for an end that never came.

Were there some Divine Creator, I concluded, His cruelty must be what drives mankind. Or perhaps there was no creator but mankind. Fearing insignificance, they designed gods to bless them with control over all, to assure them death was not merely the closing of an eye, a blink in time, nothing more.

If death were just the end of consciousness, if mankind were nothing special for their sentience, why should I be denied this final rest? What weight had any penitent promise I made?

And if some Divine Creator should hold me accountable for my sins? What worse suffering could He impose?

Nothing. *Nothing*, I thought then.

But am I not the inheritor of Frankenstein's sins, blessings, and consequences? He rationalized so eloquently. He inspired people to love him, to help in his unholy creation of me. Even as he was enthralled in the deepest madness, his friends loved him enough to risk their lives in his quest to destroy me.

Let *me* tell you of love. And promises.

***

In this frozen wasteland, sunlight upon snow can create light more blinding than the deepest hour of the month-long night. Even on the cloudiest nights, I can see. When daylight expresses brilliant tyranny, I remain inside this outpost I—no, *we*—have claimed as home.

This painful illumination feeds my greater purpose, my promise to my beloved, so long as I keep the solar panels clean. I have mastered the collection and storage of energy. No longer slave to storm or god, I am as methodical in the science of power and electricity as I am—and my creator was—in the application of chemistry, anatomy, and surgery.

Power: My creator's notes say nothing of needing electricity to awaken me. Nothing! When he created me, there was little at his disposal to generate the charge I have found necessary in recreating his experiment.

This outpost was built for scientific study. Humankind regularly attempts to reclaim it. That each attempt fails with no survivors ensures the next attempt will bring new and better tools for my application. And hope for my eventual success.

What power has Hell without hope?

But I promised to speak of love, and I digress.

My beloved mate, my dear Ingrid whom I rescued and recreated, has her own chamber during her dormancy. I would not keep her in the morgue with our human stock; she is *more* than they, as am I. She is not dead, and she is my wife. We cannot share a bed when she is in this fragile state. And even a fiend such as I would revile taking comfort in her body when she cannot respond.

It is to Ingrid's chamber I now go, for the power storage reserves are full. It takes nearly the entire year's daylight to reach this point. It has taken years to calculate the most efficient power surge for her awakening.

Last awakening, Ingrid and I shared two precious days and one sacred night, the longest duration since our original meeting. My hope—my *promise*—is that our time together never need cease.

Before I move my beloved, I examine her left shoulder and below her right knee. Gone are obvious stitches and Frankenstein's crude alchemical sealant; modern surgical thread and grafting create almost seamless transition, a complement, an *enhancement* to her already superior beauty. Assured of her body's structural integrity, I carry Ingrid to the main medical lab as a husband carries a newly-married wife over their home's threshold, as I shall bring her over the threshold between states of life.

Her flesh, though cold and hard as marble, is as smooth and fine as the artist's stone against the mummified swaths of my own skin that have not been replaced. My creator was thoughtless of my experience in this vessel; I have taken great pains to maintain the perfection of my beloved's body.

After laying her on the insulated table, I unbutton her dressing gown just enough to access the incision to the left of her sternum while maintaining her modesty. I open the incision and remove the preservatives I so carefully placed barely a year ago. Next I retrieve the heart, treated with my most recent attempt at replicating my creator's formula.

Will this time be the last time I must do this? The hope

on that question never dulls.

I connect the heart with the expertise of a surgeon who is *more than* human, one with nearly a century's practice, needing minimal rest and pause for sustenance.

Once her heart is meticulously secured, I apply the cathodes. I inhale and exhale slowly, anxiously, though my work is nothing short of perfection. I rebutton her dressing gown and kiss her on the forehead. She has said she feels my kiss in those moments between waking and sleeping; she says that kiss carries my love to her consciousness.

A bolt of lightning was the dramatic kiss that woke her from true death the first time. Today, I click a small switch between my thumb and forefinger. The facility's lights go out so quietly I hear her first gasp.

Though this compound has no windows, outside the sun rises for this season-short day. I planned her awakening for this; her appreciation of poetry is equal to mine. LED candles create a romantic glow upon a timer's command.

I caress her face, stroking her golden curls as she returns to consciousness. When Frankenstein woke me into being, I met only terror and revulsion. She should experience only love.

She leans into my touch as her breathing evens. My beloved smiles and kisses my hand just before opening her eyes.

I do not flinch when she looks at me, though the definition and clarity of her sky-blue eyes have taken on the watery, glassiness of mine. I suspect it is a side effect of my creator's chemical compound; nothing else has deteriorated. Regardless of their appearance, she sees as well as I, better than any human, and I find her no less beautiful.

For her eyes hold the same love I carry in mine.

She clears her throat and tests her voice. Like mine, it

has a rasping breathiness. She speaks in the song of an antique violin.

"You've done it again, beloved. You've done it again." She rewards my efforts with her lips upon mine, renewing our vows of nearly a century.

***

1944

My cursed existence would have me return to the lands of man when the world was at war. As insult upon injury, I would learn that not even a century's progression of war machines could end me.

Initially unaware of the battle-scarred landscape to the south, I first went to Scotland's Orkney Isle—where my creator had assembled, discarded, and interred my intended mate—to find and procure Frankenstein's tools and chemicals. In my vengeful stalking of Frankenstein, I had committed to memory all the man's correspondence. My mind held a narrated map of names and places where I might find more clues to solve the mystery of my unmaking. Mourning the unbirth of my intended partner, I decided that my remains should lie with hers. Feeling a semblance of peace, I continued my quest on mainland Europe.

I was incorrect to assume nothing could be more wretched than an awakened consciousness entrapped in ice. Worse still: a landmine rendered me limbless and helpless in the mud of human blood and excrement.

My supposition of the inherent cruelty of a Divine Creator, if such existed, changed only in realizing the *depth* of universal brutality. Yet my belief more readily accepted the *actuality* of Divine Consciousness; only a Divine Consciousness would write the sadistic irony that befell me.

To maintain sentience whilst trapped in a shattered and scattered body was horror enough, yet my head and torso had the fortune of being collected by what I can only conclude was an incarnation of my creator. Once more, the limbs of various corpses were attached to my body. This house of science, however, was also ornamented in Pagan runes and symbols I knew from literature. And observers! Adorned in dress suits and uniforms as if attending an elite theatre performance!

The deliciousness of their dissolving applause when I snapped the false creator's neck! The rapture of their hysteria when I turned on them!

Though I was then ignorant of the extent of their war crimes, a part of me I dare consider related to a soul *understood*: I was but a single showcase in a menagerie of depravity.

Of my actions that day, I regret only that some escaped my feral wrath.

After finding my bag of Frankenstein's work and tools —and adding to it those of this mad doctor—I fled that laboratory. In my travels, I obtained more durable clothing and a rucksack in which to carry my growing research. Commanders quickly learned the limit of their soldiers' courage and morale when bullets proved ineffective against a monster faster and stronger than any human.

I learned to dress my wounds and give myself blood transfusions when I sustained too much damage. When a building collapsed by bombs trapped my right arm, I severed it to escape and exchanged it for one from a soldier's corpse pinned under an overturned AGDZ. The success of that operation, and the greater utility of the new limb, led me to replace the rest of my extremities. The showman doctor who rebuilt me, while using fresher parts than Frankenstein had access to, had not collected the best specimens of humanity.

But I chose my battles carefully. I know not the extent

humans feel pain, but I do suffer from it, and what intelligence would willingly endure such misery without the promise of death's final freedom?

I made my way to Ingolstadt, where Frankenstein had first learned the secrets of my creation. From there, I sought the secrets of my utter and complete destruction. How and where I traveled, seeking artifacts of Frankenstein's academic Odyssey—over a century past—is of little matter. I obtained the knowledge to accomplish the events in my tale of love.

But not enough to evade the more damnable consequences.

***

As I serve my beloved Ingrid breakfast, she grabs my most-recently acquired hand with a gasp. "What's *this*?" The disgust upon her lips sends an unexpected twist through my stomach.

I yank away as if she struck me.

She softens at my reaction, but doesn't smile. "That *colored* flesh...It doesn't become you. Your hand should complement your status, your intelligence...your *greatness*."

I glance between the arm and her, flexing and fanning the long, dark fingers. I took it from the commander of the most recent attack upon our home. He'd distracted me from my protected position and destroyed my former forearm with a well-aimed explosive. As formidable an opponent as any human could be, he was a strong specimen that would make me stronger.

"Don't fret about it now, beloved," Ingrid says, offering me her celestial smile. "We've been parted too long. Let's eat. Later, I'll help you change that appendage for a more worthy one. Surely more human *offerings* have been sent to try and unseat us from our temple." She chuckles at her reference to our godlike state; I do not argue. She is Persephone to my Hades, and I endeavor to smite every pomegranate seed that keeps her from my company.

I return to the table, taking her hand in my paler one, and kiss her knuckles. With the same unnatural speed and grace, she pulls my hand to her lips and returns the affection. Warmth I experience no other time than with her, warmth that doesn't bring decomposition, dances up my arm and settles like a dove in my heart.

"You have advanced even in your cooking, my love." The bliss crossing her face heats me elsewhere than my heart, and I anticipate the ecstasy of later affections.

"In one of the invading human's electronic book collections, I found several volumes on food." I lower my eyes in the coy way she does when she wishes to impress me. "I wanted to make our time together even more satisfying to your senses."

"Mmmm..." She moans as she chews slowly, sensuously.

My desire for her as my wife grows physically uncomfortable and compelling. I stop eating that I might visually feast upon her.

Ingrid looks at me through her lashes as she swallows and smiles. "I appreciate your dedication to my pleasures. Have you also found research that prolongs the pleasure of my time with you?"

I admire the deep intellect behind her gaze. "I hope that I have. Do you feel any different with this awakening?"

Putting her utensils on her cleaned plate, Ingrid stretches her back against the chair so her well-formed breasts reach heavenward, still hard from death's chill or erect in expectation of what I hope is an immediate repose to our shared bed. It takes me a moment to attend to her spoken response: "I believe I do feel more vigor than I have before." She stands, stretching further. "We should test that, of course. Rigorously."

I need no further enticement to leave my unfinished meal and embrace her.

Ingrid stops me and pulls my sleeve past the seam attaching my new forearm. Touching only the paler flesh, she guides me not to the bedroom but to the morgue and its adjoining medical area.

"But first, my beloved, let's make sure all of you is aligned with your greatness."

***

1944

"Put your hands in the air." The voice was female and unafraid.

I complied out of curiosity. I'd just climbed down a hole through a demolished office building, seeking shelter from a snow storm. The woman could clearly see me; the rifle click echoed an accurate aim. It had been…a very long time…since I had conversed with a woman. Longer since that interaction was not one of terror.

"Turn around."

With a sigh, I did so, prepared to rush and disarm her upon the immediate panic I expected. German troops were retreating from this village, which had been hollowed out by the prior evening's air raid. I had hoped for sheltered respite while I scavenged for more food and potable water.

She did not panic. Nor was her face overtaken with revulsion and abhorrence. The drawing of her brow and lips, the scrunching of her delicate nose just behind the rifle butt revealed only a mild disgust, wariness, and—most surprising—intrigue. "What are you?"

A shock of air burst from my nose and mouth. It took me a moment to recognize it as a laugh.

"You find that question funny?" she asked, unwavering

in her grip on the rifle.

I studied my apparent captor. She knelt behind the remains of an auspicious-looking desk. Her head covering was that of a nurse, but she faced me as a soldier: unwitting that a gunshot would not slow me.

"I do." My voice croaked; I could not recall the last time I'd spoken aloud. For her part, she waited patiently, gun steady, while I collected myself and warmed up my vocal chords. I finally finished, "Find your question funny."

The rise of her golden eyebrows demanded further explanation.

The interaction excited me in a way I had not felt for longer than a human lifetime. I *wanted* to speak with her, to communicate with the mind behind those sharp, sky-blue eyes that saw a monster—a massive construct of corpses with drowned eyes—and demand he explain his very existence.

I tried to better enunciate: "I find your question funny because you face me and request the one answer I cannot provide to even myself."

She squinted at me. "What is your business here?"

"The damage to this structure led me to conclude, incorrectly I see now, that it would be uninhabited and, therefore, a safe place to rest until this snowstorm passes." I gestured to the hole where snow fell upon the rucksack I'd dropped in before I'd descended.

Her deepened consternation suggested my response was not what she'd expected. "You are not Wehrmacht. That uniform you wear isn't yours."

I looked from her to the uniform that barely held together against my largeness. "No," I said. "I took it from the last person who aimed their gun at me."

The rifle barrel quivered, accompanied by a poorly hidden gasp.

"I have no need of women's clothes, so if you reposition your rifle away from me, I won't come any nearer while I rest." Though I was loathe to leave her company, rifle or not, I also offered, "Or I could find another building for shelter before I continue my own journey."

The nurse did not reposition her rifle. "And just where might your own journey be taking you?"

"Scotland." Thrills danced up my spine as our conversation continued. "I return to the Orkney Isles specifically."

"And what's your business in Scotland? What's in the Orkney Isles?"

"Very little but hovels. And the body of one who was promised to me." Did I intend to be coy in my answer? I could not honestly say, but the thought of our interaction ending had grown nearly as painful as a bullet wound.

"I'm sure there's more than that." She spoke with a sneer, but that did not deter me.

"Oh yes, there is. But that is a very long story, and it is tiring to stand here with my arms in the air." That was my first lie to the woman. The effort engaged in complying with her initial words did not tire me in the least; it was just an aggravation. "Would it so inconvenience you to put down your weapon?"

"It *would* so inconvenience me to allow you space to assault me. And even if you've the honor to not attack a woman, I couldn't allow a potential spy to 'carry on with his journey' to Scotland or wherever you may truly be going."

"You think I am a spy?" I was delighted with her accusation; did she really assume I was some ugly, oversized agent for other parties in this war?

Had she just allowed me that measure of personhood?

"I don't know what you are but one who casually

confesses to the murder of my countryman and theft of his belongings."

I took a step closer, studying her face.

Her eyes were clearly focused as she moved her finger from alongside the barrel to the trigger. "I will shoot you. You would not be the first man I killed, nor even the second or third."

"And you would not be the first woman I killed, nor the second or third either. But I truly do not want to harm you." Bored with my submissive charade, I lunged.

Her shot was immediate and accurate. The bullet went straight through me. Were I human, my death would have been instant. Instead, I stumbled, slowed indeed, reeling in pain as my torn heart pumped blackened blood and fluid down my front and my back.

How I live through such mortal wounds, my creator's notes never revealed. I would shortly fall into a torpor to heal; I would be weakened and pained until I transfused more blood, ate, and drank fresh water. I had but moments to kill her or convince her to not abuse me in my coming unconsciousness.

Now horror crossed her face. And...awe. As I barely held myself erect before her, she reached as if to caress my wound. "How is this possible?" she asked.

I had neither wit nor strength to answer. More pertinently, the last moments of consciousness revealed her choice to face me was not entirely of courage or intrigue. Her foot and calf were crushed beneath a pile of rubble, hidden—along with a corpse of a soldier, likely the original owner of the rifle she'd just shot me with—behind the massive, ornate desk.

My final observation, as I slumped upon that space between us, was that she not once looked upon *me* with fear.

***

Ingrid runs marble-pink fingers over my new forearm
and hand, this one nearly as pale as hers. She kisses the
seam, still visible for its recentness. Her breath is heavy
from our lovemaking, ragged from the cries I urged from
her being. I am trembling as I lie in our bed, not recovered
enough to evaluate if she indeed has more vigor than usual.

"Have you ever found me with child while I am in
torpor?" she asks.

"No," I answer. "I could not have hidden such an
event." After we share our marriage bed, we have always
done a thorough examination of her body, including
ultrasounds and X-rays of her internal torso. We would
have seen such a development.

She snuggles against me, unflinching as her perfect
breasts, now supple and soft, press against my sallow, rough
chest. "Have you ever studied my reproductive system while
I…was not awake?"

I scowl. Does she think I might violate her so while she
was indisposed?

But her visage holds no accusation, only curiosity that
flashes to surprise and offense. "Do you *not* wish to have
children with me?

"I do," I assure. "I only never considered examining you
while you were not awake to know what I was doing."

"Why not?" When I do not answer—I cannot explain
why I find such an act repulsive—she adds, "I do not feel
pain when I am in that state. I would not suffer any study."

I am still speechless. That we might have children—
that she would have my children—the very thought brings
indescribable euphoria. Yet that is not how I feel.

"If my awakeness does not last this time, do so. See if
there is decay or damage to my reproductive organs; ensure
your revitalizing alchemy has preserved those parts. And if

you find any deformation or imperfection..." My beloved makes a face as if ill. "Some of the missions to steal our home have included women, no? See if any have parts in better condition. And if so, give them to me." Then, she adds, "But only so long as the woman *is* a good specimen. Do not give me the womb of a colored woman or a Jew."

I nod and kiss her forehead, though I feel emotions foreign to love.

She settles against me once more. "We should populate our domain with the most perfect children."

***

1944

I awoke from torpor between the woman who shot me and the corpse of the soldier she likely also shot. Upon finding her sleeping form against mine, I defied the aching sluggishness of temporary rigor mortis to pull away. Far enough that I might see if she had violated me beyond the gunshot wound.

I only managed cursory examination when her soft and ragged moan yanked back my attention. She sat up with similar rigid pain and stared at me. Bruised rings underlined cerulean eyes, which had grown paler, and she squinted, revealing crinkles of dehydration. "You live," she croaked through parched lips.

"In a manner," I said after a pause to keep my speech from slurring. "I do not die, in any case."

Cringing as she attempted to swallow, the woman looked between the dead man and me. "You cannot die?"

I shook my head. My heart beat beneath a scar fresher than the papery yellow skin of my chest. I found no evidence of either harm or healing by the nurse's hand and was relieved at the absence of both. Pressed with the weight of her gaze and the question hanging between us, I replied, "I have thus far found that to be true. And that is my business in the Orkney Isles; I return there in hopes of finding and executing my demise."

Her eyes widened in a shade of horror I did not comprehend. "Why *ever* would you do such a thing?"

I had no answer for her, or rather, I had too many. Disarrayed by physical discomfort, I could not assemble my thoughts.

A wild fervor fueled her words. "You have what all mankind seeks, what they aspire to, what they'd sacrifice their own gods to attain, and you seek its *demise*?"

Unable to validate my decided course of action, I pushed myself to my feet and limped toward my snow-coated rucksack. "I need food and water, and so do you—"

Feral laughter clawed from her mouth and darted through the ruins like a swarm of bats exposed to sun. I glanced up and out the hole outside, not eager to face any soldiers potentially within earshot; I perceived no life besides my cackling companion.

After the last rabid chuckle fluttered from her lips, she said, "Oh, my strange friend, I am well beyond what food and water can repair. Does your undying nose function? Can you not smell the putrescence spoiling me? Unless your bag also carries the secret of your immortality, you would waste your supplies to share them with me."

Little did she know how closely her words brushed against truth. But I was intent on my hallowed destruction. I retrieved my sack and sat nearer to her.

I did smell putrescence; I had become accustomed to its ever-present stench in this damned warzone. But she was right; it was stronger here—and it did not come from the dead soldier. The cold air of winter's lingering days had slowed his decomposition.

I studied her crushed leg. Infection's yellow pus soaked the deflated pulp within her stocking. No doubt gangrene stained her flesh with active death. I wished otherwise, but I knew the pain she bore. Even as I admired her fortitude in such agony, I envied her ability to end it.

I nodded to the rifle she still clutched. "Are you out of bullets? Perhaps the pistol still in his holster is loaded."

The contempt in her glare hit like a blow. "If Death should defeat me, its victory will not come by my surrender." She drew the gun closer as if she feared I would take it and hasten her enemy's triumph.

I drank from a canteen I'd pulled from my bag. The thirst in her eyes pulled upon my reconstituted heart and, I confess, excited me with a sense of power. I held the canteen within her reach and said, "Did you not just tell me it was a waste to give you food or water? How is that not surrender?"

She loosened her hold on the rifle to snatch the canteen. A peculiar sensation flitted from where our fingers nearly touched. Upon draining my canteen dry, crystal sharpness returned to her eyes. "And you...You did not contradict my wondering if you carried the secret to your immortality along with food and water. Or did I miss it in my delirium?"

I pulled a second canteen from my bag, the last I had, drinking half before passing it to her. My heart pounded in anticipation of that momentary nearness, rewarded with an even stronger flight of energy from my fingertips to my chest. I required a moment to compose myself before responding, "I have known you for only a short time, but you strike me as one who misses very little, even in the throes of delirium."

"And you strike me as one who knows Death well enough to be wise enough not to discard the treasure of conquering mortality."

When she handed back the canteens, our fingers

brushed. I was overtaken by a shiver of that phantom palpation—a thing I had never experienced in all my abject existence: pure pleasure. Once more, my sentience was taxed to reply to her more sober observation. My dedication to my own unmaking was bewildered by the insemination and conception of this new emotion. To hide my violently tilting apperception, I studied the can of meat I pried open. "You have no idea of the wisdom I possess that contradicts your assumptions of any treasure immortality offers."

"Then enlighten me, my wise new friend," she said. This second address of me as a "friend" stole back my full attention. Having never seen such an expression directed at me, I did not recognize the seduction in her smile. "While you regain your strength for travel, while I continue my personal war against Death, tell me your story. But if you'd kindly indulge a woman fighting for her life...Allow me to offer you a delirious bargain?"

My heart shook with yet another new and foreign feeling. It was all I could do to not choke on two words. "I'm listening."

"If, when your tale is done, I still live and am unconvinced of your conclusion to destroy yourself...and if you do hold in your lap the secrets of immortality, give me the chance to discover for myself the wisdom you claim to have. Gift to me the treasure you would throw away! Let me learn its worthlessness by my own devices." Her eyes shone with the brightness reserved for the most holy and unholy—and the sun upon a world of snow and ice.

In that moment, I understood why my creator broke his promise and destroyed my intended mate. Here was one who would be my equal, my partner, asking me to give her —to *gift* her—my wretchedness, and here was I, hesitating, balking at such an absurd opportunity.

She understood my silence with perfect clarity. With

keen intellect, she tempted with an eloquence Satan, himself, would envy. "I see a loneliness in you that would make angels cry. I imagine the existence of one with no equal…might invite despair to trick him into believing relief lies only in his own destruction. You said you were returning to Orkney…to the body of one promised to you. Did you once share this life with another? I have watched a soldier wounded, but not mortally, surrender to death upon hearing his fiancée had died. Is that what drives you to seek your end?"

From beneath her skewed nurse's cap, disheveled golden curls haloed a face of unspoken promise rivaling anything a devil might offer a starving messiah in a desert. Her words alone unmade me in a way no science or unholy alchemy could ever do.

As she spoke, she'd reached not for the food I offered, but for me. Unflinchingly—eagerly, even!—she clasped her hand over mine and transferred a vitality my creator failed to instill.

In that small affection, two epiphanies struck me with the acuity of Divine Truth.

First, nothing I said would deter her desire for that which I so despised in myself.

Second, I would dedicate my existence no longer to my destruction but to the fulfillment of her deepest desire.

I was ignorant to the spectrum of consequence inherent in such flashes of omniscience.

***

It nears a century's passage since I met my Ingrid in that bombed-out building. Yet the days we have spent together in sentient wakefulness comprise but a few months.

My time interacting with other humans, those that wish to reclaim our haven, has eclipsed the time shared with my beloved. Though undying, I am not immutable—beyond replacing injured appendages. Beyond even the conflicts, some of which have sparked unexpected esteem for our assailants. I devour every piece of literature scavenged from their invasions. I listen to their audio recordings. I deconstruct and reconstruct their technology that I might master it. I dissect and study the ever-diverse collection of corpses, seeking that eternal spark my creator gave but did not record: That evades me to this day, thwarting my shared immortality with she who I love above all.

I am no longer the being she met during her personal war against Death.

The stasis holding her captive for but a few days each year has preserved her *self* as well as her body. She *is* the same person I reclaimed from the threshold of death.

After we examine Ingrid's body, particularly her reproductive organs, and find nothing deformed or decayed, we sit upon a couch in a common room and share stories we have not yet told during our brief reunions.

"Did I ever tell you how I happened to be in that building when you found me?" She leans against me as she delicately sips coffee.

"You were trapped under a collapsed ceiling."

When she raises a brow at me, I smile—my death-black lips line perfect teeth.

Unrepulsed by my mismatched grin, Ingrid laughs, seeing only my jest. "I was interviewing for a job. I'd be caring for children—strong examples of the best in humanity—who had been liberated from inferior families. I was to be part of a team to ensure their health and retrain them for placement with families of superior heritage."

A discomfort twists my intestines; my mirth fades. Something I cannot define feels *wrong*.

"Perhaps," she says, "if we discover our immortality doesn't allow for my reproductive abilities—or if we require extended time to unlock the secret of natural reproduction for ones such as ourselves…Perhaps we could do similar."

"'We could…do similar'?"

"Venture from here. Find superior children with inferior families, and bring them into our home. Once you've perfected the science of your immortality, we could make them like us."

"'Make them like us…'" I eliminate agreement or discord from my tone with surgical precision; I fail to hide the nausea her suggestion affects in me.

As she silently turns her coffee cup in her hands, the betrayal on her face knifes at my heart.

I tuck a curl behind her ear. "I much prefer the thought of us creating our own children. Your beauty while pregnant, I imagine, would make Venus jealous."

A smile returns to her lips and she kisses my caressing fingers.

We have been denied the time to grow and change together, and I am only now seeing the consequence of that reality.

***

1944

My beloved died when I removed her gangrenous leg.

Or so I thought.

I employed all the tools and knowledge I'd collected to replace it with that of the dead soldier preserved by the cold. She awoke a day after the surgery. A day after that, she had mastery over the replaced limb.

She told me her name was Ingrid Schulz, and she had, in fact, killed the soldier whose leg she now wore.

"He wears the clothes of your countrymen," I remarked.

"A lie. My true countryman would not have propositioned me as he did."

While she gave me her name, I did not give mine. I'd long decided none fit me. She asked if she could call me "friend." Later that name became "beloved."

Ingrid convinced me go with her to one of the facilities where her countrymen practiced the "natural philosophy" my creator studied. Though disgusted by the doctor who had worked upon me before an audience, I agreed; my desire for her company overruled all else.

A week into our travel, signs of decay resurfaced in her leg, a development I had never experienced. She theorized that despite halted breathing and heartbeat, she had not entirely crossed the threshold of death, and that prevented complete integration of the foreign flesh. Rather than test that theory with her death, she proposed we try alterations to Frankenstein's chemical proportions with a fresh appendage.

I was searching for supplies on the other side of a slaughtered encampment when I heard Ingrid call out. I ran, anxious her limb had failed. Or worse, I had failed in staving off her mortality. I found her enthusiastically enrobed in gore, holding a bone saw and a freshly harvested leg. The leg's former owner, a woman in a different nursing uniform, consciously convulsed, bound to a wooden stretcher.

"Hurry," Ingrid said. "Perhaps since I still live, if you attach this while she also breathes, our flesh will better integrate."

***

Ingrid and I dance to a song she remembers from her youth, found on one of the devices collected from trespassing humans. Impossibility courts my every sense: the salty-alkaline taste of her recently-kissed skin, the vanilla-lavender scent of her freshly washed hair, the pressure and movement of her body against mine, the music of her laughter mixing with lyrics of love, and the admiration—the affection—on her face when she looks upon me. *Me*: a daemon of corpses whose existence has driven men to madness.

This moment should be nothing but perfection, but I am unsettled with the physiology of indigestion from the prior day's discussion of stealing children.

When the song ends, she asks yesterday's other disturbing question: "Have you ever studied my reproductive organs when…I was not awake?"

The heartache draws at my face more clearly than words can convey. I have failed; dread poisons the little time we have left before I must end this awakening.

Her expression shatters in mirrored sentiment. She turns away as if ashamed, and her voice trembles around her words. "I'm forgetting again, aren't I?"

I embrace her and rest my lips on her head. Forgetfulness signifies her sentience deteriorating despite my efforts. She is dying again. Tears sting my eyes and nose.

She wraps her arms around me, turns, and kisses up my arm. "It's happened just now, no? Well into evening on our second day together? Nearly a day's improvement from last time! You *will* discover the secret to our everlasting romance. Fret not, my beloved." She kisses my face. "What burden is patience for those of us who are eternal?"

I meant to comfort her with my affection, yet she comforts me. How could this not be a more perfect love?

***

1944

Ingrid's theory of a still-living replacement proved false. But rotting limbs became an inconsequential concern.

My beloved Ingrid unquestionably died during an air

raid near the Russian border.

I found her buried in debris, missing the entirety of her left arm. Her angelic face sagged, bereft any life. Not even a trickle of blood fell from the gaping hole at her shoulder.

I laid her body and a fresh arm upon an altar within the crumbled remains of a church. I employed every note and tool and combination thereof I'd found or stolen. With each day I failed to bring her back, depression devoured my life, save for the tortured awareness of her absence.

In that darkest moment of existence, my contemptuous faith swayed further toward the existence of a most cruel Divine Creator. From nowhere coalesced a storm of epic proportion, a maelstrom dwarfing every tempest of myth and literature. A lightning bolt struck the fallen church steeple and sent its charge racing chaotically over the area. Over Ingrid's body. Even I was stricken, incapacitated as flames sprouted along wooden beams and tapestries.

Ingrid's gasp resonated louder than the electrified church bells. I sprung to my feet, gathered her body—her supple and breathing body!—and carried her to safety.

We had but precious hours, our rekindled love undampened by the torrents of rain that broke from the heavens, before her mind began to slip and a deep fear painted her countenance.

Ingrid clutched my collar as if it were her salvation. "You—in your history, you-you said you awoke with no memory of who-who you were...before." She cupped my face and tapped my temple. "No idea who this brain, this face belonged to."

I shook my head and kissed her hand, pulling her close. My personality may have held fragments of the person that once carried the head I was given, but my sense of self felt entirely my own, distinct from the pieces that made me.

"I'm-I'm forgetting who I am, who I was," she sobbed. "I am losing myself. To be reborn and to not be *me*, is that not still my death?"

I had not considered that distinction, that potential when I bestowed my creator's alchemy upon her body. Would what I brought to life still be the woman I loved?

Would she still love me?

"You must solve this new challenge, my beloved. Please," she begged. "Find a way to immortalize *me* as well as my body. Promise me this?"

"I promise." I would have sworn anything to ease her distress.

She gave me a kiss of deepest sanctity. And she vowed: "Then I promise I am yours for all of my existence."

Rain couldn't camouflage my tears. "And I am yours."

We kissed once more with the consecration of matrimony. Then she unsheathed the knife I kept on my belt and pressed its hilt into my palm. "End me now, while I still remember who I am. Preserve my body, and do whatever you must to make real our eternity together. End me and awaken me until we have solved this."

Knife in hand, I froze at the enormity of what she asked—of the pledge I made. But her eyes were a lake of perfect trust.

By any Divine Creator that may exist, I would honor *this* covenant.

★★★

It is just past the dawn of what would be our fourth day, but we have begun the month of darkness. Our last day together held but a fleeting, final glimpse of daylight through an overcast sky.

Under shimmering darkness, my beloved Ingrid lay naked in the snow beneath me, unbothered by the sharp cold as I. More practical than romantic, we spend our final hours together outside to maintain her body and keep her blood from soiling our home.

"It is time," she whispers, caressing away my iced tears.

Her trembling shifts from the afterwaves of orgasm to the fear she displays only in these final moments. Though she faces it bravely, she has not developed an immunity to this plunge into the unknown. Will I keep my promise to revive her? Will some new obstacle prevent my success?

Will my time without her companionship bring back thoughts of my own demise?

I know she wonders these things; I do.

"I love you," she states. "My Victor." She has taken to calling me that in the past few years. If she has forgotten my disgust for that name, if she wants to make it a mantle of greatness, or if she references unfaltering faith in my subjugation of death, I do not know.

Being so named frees my hand to lift my knife. Perhaps *that* is her intent; this act has gotten no easier for me either.

"I love you, my wife." I kiss her and plunge my blade into her heart. Its cut aligns with the same incision I made just days ago.

After that first resurrection, I learned her heart, unlike mine, did not regenerate from mortal damage. I give her a new heart with every awakening, each treated with a different formulation of my creator's chemistry.

I carry her, as a husband carries his bride, over our home's threshold and into her chamber. I clean her, preserve her, dress her. I do not dissect her or study her reproductive organs; my nod to her request was not a promise.

As I seal the chamber, her absence sucks at my life like a vampire of myth, and I press my hand over my heart.

My own heart.

Is that my answer? My own heart that has beat for only

her these years?

My mind calculates how I might maintain consciousness to split my own heart, preserve it while I heal…Would the half removed from me regenerate for her? The science of the challenge intrigues my consciousness, stealing the space of depression, loneliness, and doubt in my skills.

But new questions infect my intellectual meditations.

Will the sharing of my own heart change who she is?

Who *is* the person I vowed to preserve?

Will it change who *I* am?

As the Divine Creator laughs in perverse paradox, I call upon Him:

Will I keep my promise of eternity to my beloved?

MARY SHELLEY'S BABY

A dream was gifted.
    A malformed monster child pulled back the curtain
    watery yellow-white eyes stared
    looking for love in his father's
    terror-filled eyes
       and found none
So she took the abomination to her breast
and let it suckle milk and blood
    and made an album of its life.

Electric mortal mystery
    and anatomy lessons from corpses
made short work of Inimmaculate Conception.
Psychology and analysis
    were the creature's
    bedtime tales.

Though her water broke
    and carved many rivers,
too many navigators
    forgot
       the sea
    that birthed their roads.

So she sits in the dark,
    still rocking her monster.

TURNPIKE MARY
ANSWERS PRAYERS

TURNPIKE MARY ANSWERS PRAYERS

The night of my high school graduation, I drove out to the Turnpike Madonna to say one last prayer for my best friend's mother.

I told my parents about where I was going; they understood. Gram even understood; it was one of her more lucid days. After the rest of my family left—right when Gram started going downhill for the day—keys and updated car papers in hand, I left for this task.

I knew this would be the last prayer I'd say for Tracy's mom, aka "Mom Fiske," because I knew the prayer would come true.

I just needed to pray for the right thing. This time.

For those who don't know Western Massachusetts, there's a shrine on the turnpike to the Virgin Mary. You can see it heading eastbound between the Palmer exit and the Sturbridge one. At night, a spotlight shines on her church-marble white form; she glows like heaven's light. According to local stories, miracles happen when people pray there. The man who erected it was fulfilling a promise he'd made if his wife survived cancer. She did, and there it is. Pilgrims are instructed to get off one of the exits and approach from the farm that owns the land she stands on. Sometimes, though, you'll see a car parked in the breakdown lane by her or pulled over just past the guardrail.

That was my plan. I'd drive, keep my eyes peeled for that small beacon after passing Exit 8, pull over, say the prayer, pay my toll to turn around in Sturbridge, and be back home in under an hour.

Maybe a full hour. It was graduation day for several schools in the region. I hadn't even gotten on the Pike and I'd already passed three speed traps.

I didn't want any more delays; it was already getting dark. I felt bad enough for having waited so long to make this particular pilgrimage and say this particular prayer. But I needed to do this alone. It probably didn't matter, but I didn't want anyone else tied to my actions. That's why I'd waited for graduation day. Gram's car would be mine; I wouldn't be borrowing it as I spoke the words I hated even thinking about.

Before I was born, my gram—the one who'd given me her car—had been diagnosed with some rare form of brain cancer. Back then, in the seventies, it was a death sentence. But my dad had said a prayer at this statue, and she didn't die. I'd heard the story more times than I can count.

***

After hearing the options of "keeping her comfortable" or try a risky, but promising trial surgery, Dad drove out to the St. Anne shrine in Sturbridge. His parents had taken him and his sister there as kids and shown them the left-behind crutches and old wheelchairs from miracle healings. On his way to pray for a miracle, the little white Virgin on the highway captured Dad's attention. He didn't know why, but he pulled over and prayed for his mom. St. Anne's was closed when he arrived. He said a prayer in the parking lot, but the vision of the highway statue stuck with him.

Gram survived the experimental surgery, but ended up...different. She would sometimes be the usual grandmotherly type, baking, teaching me old games with wooden boards, and telling stories. Then, out of the blue, she'd get angry and start screaming at me. Or worse, she'd scream at people who weren't there. I didn't know if they were ghosts or old memories or maybe invisible monsters. She never hurt me, never raised a hand to me, but she terrified me. When her outbursts and memory got so bad she had to move in with us, my parents got to experience these things themselves.

And as I grew older, I could see Gram's episodes even scared my dad.

***

As I entered the Mass Pike under the "Worcester/Boston" sign, I wondered what Dad had specifically prayed for when he'd pulled over that night. Staying in the right lane and watching my speedometer, I felt vindicated in my efforts when I saw the cruiser sitting right in the first cut-across.

My grandmother's car was as old as I was, a '78 Chrysler LeBaron. I'd been driving it since my learner's permit—about when Gram moved in with us because someone from the Greek church two towns over had called about her screaming at the priest speaking English for the ten-thirty Mass. Being allowed to use her car meant driving Gram for errands, so I got plenty of driving experience. I knew how easy it was to speed in that boat. It responded like turbo-charged silk to the slightest touch of the gas pedal.

The amount of effort to stay at the speed limit didn't stop the parade of thoughts and memories triggered by my maiden solo trip to Turnpike Mary.

My first trip to the roadside shrine was when I was six, when mom "should have died," according to doctors, from a late-pregnancy miscarriage.

***

Mom was in the shower and I had to pee, so I asked if I could use the toilet. She'd said something like "Okay," so I went in. Before I pulled down my pajama bottoms, she started screaming. Then I started screaming. Dad ran in as she fell, tearing the shower curtain with her. I'd never seen so much blood. Dad had to yell in my face to get the phone, call 911, and stay outside the bathroom.

Later, Dad drove us both out to Turnpike Mary. He let me sit in the front seat, and he held my hand as we prayed for mom to be safe. And the baby. Dad nearly forgot to mention the baby, I remember. He added something I didn't hear, but I'm pretty sure it was an "if there can be only one…" addendum. Then he ended with "Thy will be done. Amen." It felt like church.

Mom lived, but they lost the baby. It would've been a sister. When I was old enough to bleed and get Pro-Life lessons in CCD, Mom explained how she'd nearly lost me before I was born, but the doctor and the church had advised against any surgery to avoid future pregnancy. She sometimes had to visit a Planned Parenthood (in a scarf or a jacket with a hood in case people from our church were protesting there) to get her uterus scraped out when periods kept her in bed with pain.

I never asked about another brother or sister because I saw how it hurt my parents when someone else would ask.

★★★

Though things weren't great, Mom and Gram were both at the graduation ceremony.

My best friend, Tracy, and her mom were still in the hospital. Tracy had opted to not graduate, so she wouldn't have to leave her mom's side.

Thinking of Mom Fiske in the hospital, what put her there, I checked my speed again and frowned. I was going just above fifty. Too slow could get someone pulled over as much as too fast. I nudged the gas as I approached the Ludlow Plaza, where no less than three cruisers were parked.

And one of the cruisers decided it was time to get back into the speed trap game.

The cop and I approached the exit ramp's merge at the same time.

Taking deep, calming breaths, I checked thoroughly to make sure I wouldn't cause an accident and pulled into the left lane while maintaining an exact sixty-five miles per hour. The cop hovered beside me for a few minutes before finally speeding off. I moved back into the right-hand lane as his fading tail lights shifted left.

I wasn't doing anything illegal—I was eighteen and in my own car and following every traffic law—but I also knew I was a teen in a car on a graduation day. I hadn't had any alcohol that day, or ever again after that one time, but I was well aware others would be driving drunk. And I didn't want a cop wasting their time with me if they could keep some other innocent person from being hit by a drunk driver.

More importantly, Tracy and her mom didn't deserve to suffer any extra time if I got pulled over.

It was my fault Mom Fiske was in the hospital in the first place.

And my fault she was *still* there.

★★★

Our friends held an Anti-Homecoming Party last October. While we weren't going to get drunk and stupid, like the people who went to actual Homecoming parties, we did have unsupervised access to a few choice bottles. Someone handed me a drink heavy on Kahlua. It was delicious, and I drank the whole thing even though I'd driven me and Tracy to the party. When the host's parents came home early, I did not feel comfortable driving. So Tracy and I did the responsible thing. We called her mom for a ride.

Someone else, probably from a Homecoming party, made the less responsible decision. They swerved through a red light, T-boning Mom Fiske's Corolla right at the driver's door. Right on Mom Fiske. They drove off before any of us came to. I don't know who'd called for help. I vaguely remember flashing lights and recovering in the hospital.

I'll never forget not recognizing Mom Fiske when I finally saw her in the hospital bed.

When we were discharged, I asked Dad to take me and Tracy by Turnpike Mary before he even brought us home. He did, and we prayed that Mom Fiske wouldn't die. That was all our medicated and traumatized brains could manage.

***

I'd dipped to sixty and a car that looked like it had a light rack was coming up on the left. I nudged my speed back to sixty-five and breathed in relief as I saw the station wagon with the bike rack fly by.

Good. They can be speed trap bait, I thought as I took another glance around my surroundings, trying to figure how close I was to Exit 8, the Palmer exit. The statue was some miles after that, but the dark highway had few outstanding features between the exit and the statue. I didn't want to blow by or slam on my brakes to stop in time.

The green and white of a highway road sign hovered like a ghost beside the guardrail. The Palmer exit was seven miles away. Though I tried to focus on the road, on my speed, on getting to the shrine safely, the events of the past few months wouldn't allow that peace or focus.

***

Mom Fiske didn't die.

She stayed in a coma in the hospital, unresponsive. Tracy and I lived at her side whenever we weren't at school, dropping all extra-curricular activities. It would look bad for college, but we didn't care.

After the first month, visits from her aunts and uncles and grandparents dropped off. Most lived closer to Worcester or Boston. I was Tracy's only constant, lucid, companion.

In March, Tracy got notice that insurance would no longer pay for life support. Donations from the church only covered a few extra weeks, and then the doctors "pulled the plug" despite our protests.

Mom Fiske didn't die.

For hours, her chest shuddered breaths. Gurgles bubbled up her throat. She choked and gasped while her empty eyes flicked in all directions. Her body convulsed. A nurse would turn her on her side as she wretched up greenish-pink foam that smelled of sewage. One time, Tracy and I were the only ones in the room and had to do it. Mom Fiske's skin felt flabby, like raw chicken. I remember so clearly thinking, *She shouldn't be alive.*

Tracy sobbed, begged, and pleaded. The doctors had to "plug her back in," reinsert the tube down her throat and the IVs in her arm that looked like purple and white cauliflower.

Mom Fiske wouldn't die.

Tracy dropped out of school. No one in her family or mine, no one from the church could convince her otherwise. Tracy was going to lose everything: her diploma, her college acceptance, and her future.

★★★

The Palmer exit sign caught my headlights. Now I *had* to pay attention. As I passed the highway entrance ramp, a cruiser pulled on behind me. I held my tongue and held my prayers, focusing on my speed, staying in my lane, and looking for the spotlight illuminating Turnpike Mary.

The cop stayed behind me.

I bit my lip and stayed my course.

To this day, I can't tell you how many miles are between the Palmer exit and the little shrine. It might be a million.

Hyperaware as I was, I noticed the spotlight in plenty of time to safely slow down and pull into the breakdown lane. The cop followed me, and when I stopped, he flipped on his blue-and-whites.

After a moment of flashing back to waking up after the accident, I pulled myself together. I only had the time it'd take for the officer to run my plates to say my prayer. I had to pray right now.

"Dear Mary, Blessed Mother, please, please, please let Madeleine Annette Fiske, Tracy's Mom, Mom Fiske..." I had to be specific. No ambiguity. The cop was getting out of his car and I hadn't even grabbed my license and registration! "Please let her die. Let her die peacefully and pain free. And let Tracy be free. Thank you. Amen." I blessed myself as I said, "InthenameoftheFather,Son,'n' HolySpiritAmen," while rolling down my window with my left hand.

"License and registration?" The officer beamed his flashlight at me.

"Yes, sorry, officer...um...one sec..." I flailed toward my purse in the passenger seat and pulled out my license, registration, title, and the whole big packet I'd gotten to show everything was now in my name.

Tucking his flashlight under his arm, relieving some of its blinding pain that did nothing to stop the tears already falling down my face, he took my pile of stuff and fished out my license and registration.

"Theresa Agnes Chris...to..."

"Christopaulos," I said out of habit, then flinched. Was

it rude to correct an officer?

"Miss Christopaulos," he said, fairly accurately, and looked at me for an uncomfortable minute. "You're a long way from home...What's wrong?"

Tears soaked my face, and snot threatened to flow from my nose. I grabbed at the wad of clean tissues that had popped out of my purse with all the paperwork and did my best to look presentable. The officer waited patiently as far as I could tell. Finally, I said, "My best friend's mom is dying in the hospital and I just wanted to say a prayer for her. My family's said prayers here before and they came true and..." I opened and closed my mouth, but had run out of words. I wiped at my tears and nose again, awaiting my judgment.

"Have you been drinking tonight?" he asked, voice gentler than I expected.

I shook my head. "No, sir. I don't. Drink. It-it was a drunk driver that hit her." As I said it, I knew I would never drink again. I sent that thought in the direction of the statue, an added sacrifice to bolster my prayer.

The officer handed me back my license and registration. "Are you all right to go home, miss...?"

Possibly smearing more than wiping tears and snot at this point, I nodded. "Yes, sir. And my parents know I came out here. They're waiting up for me to get back safely."

"All right," he said. "My best to your friend's mom." He nodded at the statue and then me. "Have a safe drive home."

Please, please, please don't pray for her, too! I mentally screamed while thanking him as he headed back to his cruiser. After a minute, his lights turned off and he pulled away. He hadn't said it, but there was an understood "take the time you need" in his retreat. But I couldn't stay a minute longer. As I shifted into gear, I gave the brilliant white statue one last look and said my last prayer. "Please, just let her die."

I hadn't planned on telling Tracy about that last trip. I'd spent the school year watching her die in her mom's place. By graduation, Tracy was as pale and purple veined as Mom Fiske. Sobs strangled air from her lungs, and she was barely eating. I didn't know if Mom Fiske's actual death would change anything, but her continued survival was turning them both undead.

At the funeral, my parents told Tracy that I'd gone to the statue to pray again.

With a vigor impossible for her skeletal shell of body, she stormed over to me. "You didn't take me to pray at the miracle statue!" she just about shouted. "Why not? What did you say! Why-why didn't it work? Why didn't you just take me! She-she might…"

"I-I'm sorry…" I stammered and mumbled. "D-don't know…I-I wasn't thinking." I wasn't thinking, but I wasn't sorry. My prayer had been granted.

"No, you weren't," she spat. "How could you be so selfish?"

One of her aunts pulled Tracy away, looking at me like I were a vile rat, not the person who'd spent every possible hour in the hospital with her best friend and her best friend's dying mom. More time than that contemptuous aunt had spent.

But I was selfish. I'd wanted Mom Fiske to stop suffering, that was true, but even more, I'd wanted my best friend back. I'd prayed for Mom Fiske to die so Tracy could be free, be free to be my friend again.

That night or early morning after the funeral, Tracy borrowed some family member's car. She drove out to the shrine. By herself.

The morning news reported a major accident on the Mass Pike, eastbound, between Palmer and Sturbridge. All traffic lanes were closed, and there was a fatality. A teenaged girl they didn't name.

I knew it was Tracy. I knew she probably had prayed to be with her mom again. And the prayer was answered.

Just like mine. I'd prayed for Mom Fiske to die, for Tracy to be free. I hadn't prayed for Tracy to *live*.

My prayer to the Blessed Madonna of the Highway, Turnpike Mary, wasn't just my last prayer for Mom Fiske. It was the last prayer I'd ever dare make.

I AM MY OWN MOTHER

I planted my own egg
    of my own idea
    of my own identity
inside my womb.

I nourished her with my blood,
    rocked her to sleep in amniotic tears,
    played her lullabies with my heartbeat,
    sang her into being with my labored screams.
I gave birth to myself.
I cradled her in my arms,
    let her smear afterbirth on my face.
I permitted no doctor to spank air into her lungs.

The world pointed,
    with needles and knives.
The world aimed to tattoo "A"
    for "Abomination" on our forehead,
    on the breast
of me and myself.

I and myself escaped, hid, and rested
    in space tubes of dark rainbow windows,
    tucked between fifth and sixth dimension,
    with dark matter and dark energy
and debated dark existences.

I and myself wait,
     donned in a party dress of tangled, infinite strings of
possibility,
to be born once more
into a world ready to accept my reality.

SWAMP GAS AND FAERY LIGHTS

SWAMP GAS AND FAERY LIGHTS

She flickered her lights to life upon hearing the child's cries.

"Is someone there?" Within the choral din of crickets and frogs, footsteps squished through the mud and splashed in puddles. "Help me! Please! Someone? Oh! Oh!" A *pop* followed a loud sucking sound was followed by a wail louder than the nearby bullfrog. "My shooooe!"

She consciously flickered her lights even brighter.

"Hello? Who's there? Can you help me?" *Squish. Splash.* "Please?"

"Are ye lost, child?"

"Yes! Yes!" *Splash. Squish.* "Who's there? I've run away from my family." *Squish. Splash.* "They're awful. And now I'm lost. And I lost my shoe. Can you please help me?"

"I can help. Follow me voice…We'll find each other."

"Okay…" *Splash. Splash.* "Where-Where are you? The water is deeper here…"

"I'm here. Where are ye? Can ye follow the light? I can't see ye."

Splash. Splash. Splash. SPLASH! "Oh! Oh, no! It's deeper here! Help! Help, I'm stuck! Can you see me?"

"Ach, there ye are, child." She didn't *see*, as humans did, but she recognized the erratic movement and the essence of a foreign being in her swamp. She surrounded the flailing human girl with her flickering, dancing lights. "It appears ye are right stuck. And sinking, too."

"What-what are you? Help me, please?"

"What am I, eh? Has this generation forgotten *all* the tales? Well, back home I had the much more lovely name of Will 'o' Wisp. Here..." She sighed, her lights dimming. "Here, they call me Swamp Gas. How's that fer respect?"

"Help me, Will 'o' Wisp? Please?"

"Well, ye see, I haven't any physical form, so I can't right pull ye out..."

"But you said you could help! You said to follow your voice and you'd help!" The swamp water continued to bubble and splash with the fallen girl's writhing.

"I didn't quite expect ye to fall into one of the deep areas. Will 'o' Wisps can lead people to safety..."

"Is there any-any*thing* you can do? Please?" The girl forced words through sobs.

"There is one thing...but no. No one would ever want to do that...Perhaps I can glow brighter and someone will find ye in time."

"No. No they won't. No one's looking for me. Please, what is the one thing? I don't want to die, Will 'o' Wisp!"

"It's not a good idea, really. Ye're young. Even if ye did die, yer god promises ye a good afterlife, donna he?"

"That's what they say in church...but please—please! I'm sinking!"

"Thrashing's nah going t'help ye much, lass. Ye'll just sink faster."

The girl stopped struggling and sniffled. "What is it you think might help me? Please?"

"Ach, lass. What's yer name, dear?"

"Emma."

"Emma, child, the only way I can help ye is if ye wanted to take my place here. And give me yer life."

"I-I don't understand. Then you'd be stuck in my place."

"The switch would let both us have a touch of faery

power—just fer a few minutes. I might be able to pull yer body out with that. But ye'd be stuck as I am. Just floating lights. Nothing but pretty swamp gas…"

"I-I don't want to die, though."

"Emma…" She pulled her lights closer around the girl. "I'm going to let ye in on a little secret. Did ye know faerie don't have souls? If we switch places, ye'll lose yer soul. Ye don't want that, do ye?"

"I-I don't know. Will you take care of-of my little brothers if we switch?"

"I would, but do ye really want to switch? I want ye to be sure."

"I'm scared, Will 'o' Wisp. But I-I think I do."

"Are ye *sure*? This is my third time asking. Yer answer is final, Emma."

"I want to switch with you, Will 'o' Wisp. I'll take your life if you take mine."

***

"Help me! Someone, help me!"

She dimmed her lights and waited, recognizing the voice.

"I know you're here. I know you can hear me!" The girl's footsteps were careful, making only small *splish* and *squash* noises in the swamp mud, hardly audible over the usual evening frog chorus. She was avoiding the deeper parts. "I found the faery and magick books under your mattress!"

"It's *your* mattress now." She flickered around the tiny form that used to be hers. "Your mastery of English has gotten better, though, but I suppose that's part of the magick in becoming who I was."

"You tricked me!"

"Wasn't that what you were planning to do to me?" She moved closer. Not seeing clearly wasn't something she'd expected, but she imagined the new Emma had at least a split lip and black eye, and worse beneath her clothing.

"I'll not watch over your brothers!"

"I couldn't have if I'd died, either."

"Don't you care about them?"

"Actually, without a soul, no. It's a wonderful feeling."

"Switch us back! Right now!"

She flickered, as if in thought, but she'd made up her mind when she'd run into the swamp—the only place she knew her parents would never follow. "No."

"You'll be stuck here forever. You'll grow tired of it. And once I'm dead, you'll have no soul to return to."

"It sucks still caring about all of them, doesn't it? Even though you're not me, you still feel it, don't you? That was the hardest part of my plan, of coming here. I mean, Cody and Deckland are innocent, and I remember feeling bad about leaving them. But those people I called 'Mom' and 'Dad'? They're monsters. And apparently still are, as I can see. They must've whooped you real good after the whole running away stunt. But you know what? When I was still human, a part of me *still wanted to love them!* How wrong is that?"

"Switch us back. Please. You'll be out of the mud. You can run away. I can guide you through the swamp safely. I know its every part."

"No. I'd say 'I'm sorry,' but that'd be a lie. I remember faery aren't supposed to out-and-out lie, right?"

"Do you really want to be stuck here forever? Nothing but 'pretty swamp gas'? You could have a future!"

"It won't be forever. It will be until I've learned every inch of this swamp, too. There will always be children running from awful homes. Especially around here. The one time DSS showed up, I could tell the woman didn't care. I'll leave when I'm ready."

"Please, how can you do this to me? You know what it's like!"

"I do. And I can. And that was your third request. I've denied you three times, and it hasn't even been three days since we switched, so you cannot request again. If you know every part of this swamp, run away yourself and start a new life." She flickered herself into darkness. The new Emma didn't move, but the new Will 'o'Wisp felt her consternation on the air around her. After a few moments, the indecision turned to resignation and she *splished* back the way she came.

The Will 'o' Wisp thought she ought to feel bad, but she did not. And that was a wonderful feeling.

HOW TO WRITE LIKE A WOMAN

I

"A Pen! A Pen!
      My Lifeblood for a Pen!"
And time.
And patience.
To wait until my neighbor sleeps
      and watch
            in a lantern-slit of light
      and cut off his hands and tongue
      while he dreams of dancing with angels.
 Then cut carefully
      two inches to the left and two ribs down.
      Remove a beating heart
      not to mark his passing
      but my hemorrhaging birth.

II

Make a finely honed blade
      new metal, old technique.

Bladedance.
      Lure with a sparkling twirl,
          bright scarves
          silky sheer seductive.

With pleasure,
     misdirect.
     He lets your blade
     inside—
so sharp he doesn't feel it
yet.

And *he* will twist
     tear open innards
     guts
and release.

Pain comes upon realization
you ended his dance
with beautiful extraction.

III

The Fallen Angel of the Broken House
     sits chained
in a
yellow wallpapered
room of her own
     that he made her.
Or so he reminds her every day.

She didn't get what she asked for
     because he misunderstood the question
or didn't listen in the first place.

How was your day, dear? he asks.

She smiles

lips only
    and asks:
Do you love me?

He looks at her,
    smirks.
    No.
Are we equal now?

She kisses him,
    bites his tongue with her teeth,
    binds telephone cord
    around him
    tight—
    so he can't speak, breathe.
Now, we are equal.

Reaching into his side,
    she breaks two ribs,
    takes his liver,
and prepares dinner
    for herself.

IV

Take a word
    with many meanings
    ambiguous
    dark
    curved
    amorphous
    and fuzzy around the edges.

    Strategically place it,

in the open,
easily forgotten…
doesn't move in a straight line.
A knight.
To know the attack, you must count squares.

Mistress
      soft, feminine, dark, hidden
      a visit in the night
            you don't tell your wife or kids about
      maybe silk, maybe leather, maybe whips or chains…
            cliché
Until you twist
      in ecstasy or agony.
Oops! I clichéd again.

Feminine master:
      a woman master,
      master over women,
      a master that is woman—
      woman and *feminine*
            still feel
            less.
They only modify
            Master.

I do not modify, so I am Master.

But you only see Mistress,
      even when
            I shred your skin,
            break your back,
            bathe in your blood—
foreplay to your writhing death.

You didn't expect I meant it.
     All for none, though.
     Mistress you call me still
expecting some sort of mercy
     you wouldn't ask for
     were you to call
     me
Master.

FIXED

FIXED

"Victoria, would you mind getting another pot of coffee? It's going to be a late night."

The engineer gritted teeth behind her smile as she left the table of men. She would break into the notes later, so she could stay updated on the new specs for the joint bearings. It was her personal mission to stay on top of this project despite Broderick's insistence upon treating her like an overpaid secretary.

Victoria Chattham hadn't been a day into this contract before realizing she was hired because she, alone, fulfilled three equal opportunity quotas: woman, Hispanic, and disabled.

She flexed the fingers of the prosthetic hand that she'd been lead engineer on. That project had lost funding almost two years ago, bankrupting the small company she'd worked for. She had at least ensured that she got the one working prototype. It had not been an entirely legal process, but it had worked.

The burnished steel coffee pot beeped. With a sigh, she carried the tray with her prosthetic hand into the board room. No one noticed how effortlessly she maneuvered the heavy tray with just one hand, placing it on the table without a drop spilled.

She fixed her attention on the presentation and frowned. "Wait, you think just a silicone coating will be enough for that projected usage?" She pointed to the list of stats on the corner. "Are you crazy?"

"The manufacturer specs—" Alan Garrison, Chief Mechanical Engineer, started to scoff.

"The manufacturer's specs are bullshit." She glared. "Read the fine print." Turning her gaze to Broderick, who appeared amused enough to lift his eyes to hers temporarily, she continued, "That coating assumes no weight bearing usage of the joint, and only single-directional usage. Per the blueprints, this joint needs to lift or move up to a hundred pounds with full rotational capabilities. That coating will be worn down and you'll have metal on metal in less than a year functioning at full capacity."

"And you know this from...tests you've run?" Garrison asked, waving a dismissive hand.

"Hijo de Diós," she muttered. "Yes, nearly seven years of testing, and then almost two years of direct usage." Unbuttoning her right shirt cuff, she folded and shoved it nearly to her shoulder. Had no one read her work? The flesh around her prosthetic was a shade lighter than the rest of her body, but only that suggested it was not the limb she was born with. She rarely wore less than three-quarter sleeves, keeping the line of difference hidden. The men in the room glanced between each other and her in confusion, except for Broderick, who stared steadily, perhaps the longest time on record without looking to her tits or ass.

Slipping her fingers under the flesh "glove," she unhooked the neural attachment that allowed almost perfect sensory simulation, then proceeded to fold the glove until her elbow and half her forearm's mechanics were exposed. She managed to subdue most of a smirk upon the gasps, and then the murmurs of admiration.

Except Mason Broderick. Broderick gave a half nod and pulled a thick file folder from under his clipboard, proceeding to pass around packets of paper.

"You were the lead engineer on *that* project, weren't

you, Ms. Chattham?"

"I was." Something in his tone chilled her, and she regretted her moment of indignant pride. She *knew* the smart thing to do was keep quiet about her arm, no matter how thorough she'd been in doctoring the history and records so it "belonged" to her.

Leaving her arm exposed—it seemed the right thing to do—she reattached the sensory cable. It took a moment for the faux skin to get used to feeling folded upon itself, but it didn't hurt. She picked up the packet and leafed through it.

Or, rather flipped through the first two pages before dropping it.

"Where did you get this, Mr. Broderick?" She tried to keep both the accusatory and panicked tone from her voice.

He gave her the slightest smile and flash of perfect white teeth below his sculpted moustache. "When the Medical Endeavors team lost their grant, I offered them an under-the-table buyout in return for all their information. It's how they could give all the laid-off employees generous severance packets."

"Interesting," was all Victoria said. Scratch the "only hired for EEO purposes" theory; Broderick was a more manipulative bastard than she'd thought.

"As you know, I handpicked this entire team," he continued. "I wanted your particular expertise on these things."

With that, every other man in the room nodded approvingly at Victoria.

"Now, Ms. Chattham." Broderick grabbed the projection screen's remote, switching the view to his own tablet. "If you would kindly refresh us on your notes regarding bionic appendages and then give me feedback on how I applied it to our team project, that would move things along."

"Of course, Mr. Broderick." For the next hour and a half, Victoria jumped between excitement about her research and terror regarding what other knowledge about her Broderick was hiding and how he would use it against her.

***

"Another long day?" Bill Chattham placed a steaming cup of chamomile in front of his wife after she checked on the two sleeping boys.

She nodded, taking the warm cup with a murmured "thank you" while trying to gauge her husband's mood and pain level.

He rubbed her shoulders. "A good day, though?" He was testing her, too. She couldn't blame him. She'd come home a right bitch more often than not lately.

"Mmmnn." Was it a good day? With one statement, her boss had elevated her from waitstaff to new Chief Mechanical Engineer. It *had* been her work that was impressive. Then again, the tone of his voice, the baiting look in his eye whenever she looked at her notes…

"'Mmmmn' isn't very descriptive," Bill teased, tipping her chair back a few inches so he could kiss her on the nose.

She squealed, grabbing his arms. "Ee! Don't *do* that!"

"Ow!"

Her chair banged back into place as he yanked his arms from her grip.

"Oh, God! I'm so sorry, Bill! I just…I don't like tipping…it feels like…" She bit her lip, fighting her mind from flashing back to the accident that had taken her arm—and nearly killed Bill.

"You don't know your own strength." He glared at her prosthetic arm.

She stood, cradling it.

Closing his eyes, he took a deep breath and leaned on

the fridge. His lips silently counted, a trick their therapist taught him.

"I'm sorry." Her voice felt tiny. Despite the brain injury that had screwed with his temper, Bill had never, ever raised a hand to her or the children. He'd lost it once, just once, and smashed the family computers. She knew in her heart he'd never hurt them. Hell, the therapy had been his idea!

He stopped counting, but still took deep breaths. He was *trying*. Victoria put her left hand, her real one, on his chest, leaning her body on his and closing her eyes. After a few moments, he wrapped his arms around her. It felt good.

No need to worry him about what Broderick might know.

***

Broderick was building a robotic suit.

Victoria sat back in her chair upon reviewing the full project stats sent to her internal email. Until now, she had only seen pieces. She knew that Broderick World Enterprises was the global leader in robotics, and that half the parts on the Medical Enterprises project were sourced from them, but she'd never, no pun intended, put the pieces together.

It seemed too ridiculous. Too much...well, too much like a particular comic book series kept in her dad's pristine cardboard-backed sleeves. Victoria had been grounded twice for raiding his collection, but he'd eventually given in and started rereading them with her when she was eleven. It had been her *big date with Daddy* when she was thirteen to go see the movie.

Normal people, rich and über-smart as they may be— and Broderick was in the top tier of rich and über-smart— *normal* people did not try and build super human-robot fighting suits.

The specs didn't actually include weapons, but they

were incomplete. There *were* various partially created plans for flight that spanned rocket fuel to electromagnetism. It was kind of scary.

It was also pretty damned exciting.

By lunch, Broderick managed to get his hands on enough supplies to let Victoria's team of mechanical engineers start mock-ups for the joints. The team *listened* to her. It was past dinnertime, again, when they had done enough testing to get optimal measurements for the software designers. After a catered evening meeting with Broderick, they had a timeline to begin simulations within six weeks.

For the first time in almost two years, Victoria drove home with a smile.

***

"It's okay, honey." Victoria stood in a puddle of water amid the triangle of her red-faced husband, two tear-faced boys, and the still-trickling dishwasher, half-yanked from under the counter. "I can fix this. I can fix anything, remember?"

"I'm sorry, baby. I-I..." Bill cast a guilty glance to Mike and Petey. Neither of them had any injuries. Bill had a gash up his forearm that still seeped blood across a deeply purpling bruise.

"Shh...sh-sh-sh." Victoria looked between them, soothing. She took a tentative step toward her husband, then put a hand on his arm. No warmth, so no infection. "Just wash this out with antibacterial soap, and I'll take a look at it, okay, babe?"

He nodded. "Vic...I..." He glanced at the boys again. "I didn't."

She stood on her tiptoes and kissed his rough cheek. "I know, babe."

Leaning his head on hers for a moment, Bill sighed.

"I'm gonna tuck in the boys. Just wash that out and have a seat, okay?" She kissed him once again before heading toward her sons.

When she returned to the kitchen, Bill was *not* resting in a chair, but on his hands and knees, sweatpants soaked three quarters of the way up, mopping water and suds.

"I can get that—"

"You worked all day." His arm swept across the floor with the zeal of one slaying enemies with a dishtowel.

Victoria knew better than to argue; she knew the lines they'd say by heart. Taking a deep breath, she grabbed a chamois from under the sink. "Mikey really likes the manga you got him. He'll probably be exhausted tomorrow because he'll read through this one tonight."

Her husband sagged a little as she knelt beside him, and she almost melted from the gratitude in his eyes and the silent question of why she even put up with him. Picking up his towel and tossing it into the sink, where it landed with a *sploosh*, she edged closer and took his injured arm. Kissing his knuckles, she asked, "Can I see this now?"

Darkness touched his face again, though he relaxed his arm. "I *know* how to bandage a cut."

"I know you do. Doesn't stop that crazy mom instinct from wanting to check every little injury on my boys." He had, in fact, done a good job of layering sterile pads up his arm and neatly taping each overlap. Being the stay-at-home parent to two boys, since even before the accident, meant that Bill knew his way around the medical shelf in the linen closet. Victoria lightly kissed the bandage. "See, you couldn't do that yourself."

He smiled again, blue eyes hinting the playful spark she'd loved from the moment she met him. "No, you're right. That wouldn't work if I did it."

"All right, what I need is the area closest to the washer

dry. Can you work on that while I get my toolbox and change real quick?"

He nodded. When she returned in her "dirty work" sweats and a so-worn-it-was-almost-see-through Batman T-shirt, heavy toolbox clutched in her prosthetic hand, cordless drill in her flesh hand, the area around the dishwasher was just about bone dry and the rest of the kitchen floor had only sheen of leftover dampness. Bill grinned from the floor. "Good enough?"

"Perfect."

Victoria removed the front panel so she could access the internal motor. She really didn't need the tools or the drill. It wasn't a plumbing problem; a quick glance below the sink when she had grabbed the chamois informed her the pipes and hoses were intact despite Bill's hulkish moment. It wasn't electrical either, thank God. Not that she couldn't have fixed that just as easily—her talents seemed to best manipulate current or charge issues—but that would be dangerous with all the water.

The motor for one of the blades was stuck. Victoria only needed to touch, caress even, the molded plastic above the motor to feel it, feel the life of the machine—which she knew sounded crazy, so she only thought this way to herself —and coax it to work. When she felt the mechanism was fixed, she reassembled the front panel and realigned it. Closing the dishwasher, she regarded the crack through the countertop that would have been outdated when she was a child.

She felt her husband's tense body behind her. Victoria tried to mask her own deep breath. "If we just can edge it back in, it'll be fine," she said. "Then just epoxy the crack for now. My job is going good, so we'll be caught up on the bills, and we can start getting those renovations we planned."

He didn't say anything, but skinny as he was, he moved her out of the way with his body and muscled the washer back in place.

"We can just have the contractors start in the kitchen…" She continued her pep talk as if her husband wasn't doing exactly what his physical therapist had told him not to. If she pointed it out, he'd only push harder.

Bill grunted, not meeting her eyes. The red on his too-pale cheeks and the tight lines around his eyes confessed more pain than she knew he wanted to let on. Trying not to limp, he grabbed the epoxy from the broom closet and sealed the crack with the same precision as he'd bandaged his arm.

They finished cleaning up together before retiring to just an hour of television before Victoria had to go to bed for her next early morning.

★★★

"Why is it that it seems only *you* can make the joints work correctly, Ms. Chattham?" Mason Broderick glanced between the armor on his arms and legs and the woman making minute adjustments.

Victoria pressed her lips into a tight smile, not missing the layer of acid concealed below his joking tone. "I've worked on joint mechanics longer than anyone else on the team, sir. And my day-to-day life kind of depends on it."

"I see."

Her stomach turned. She'd never planned on getting this close to her boss, but once he'd put on the armor, the joints seemed to lose their fluidity. Proximity was only half of her discomfort. The mechanical team was stuck on this part when the prosthetics project lost its funding. Same problem. The joints only seemed to respond with proper sensitivity to Victoria.

She was basically puttering around Broderick at this

point. In her mind, she was coaxing the machinery to respond to his body, pick up on nerve sensors they'd so carefully tuned to his physiology. She sensed some other signal not coming from the armor. She couldn't pinpoint it, but not having encountered it her prior projects, she dismissed it for the moment; she could investigate it later.

In a voice so low only she could hear, he said, "I never realized that just tightening and loosening the plating screws had so much effect."

"Amazing, isn't it." She allowed herself a moment of pride at how neutral she kept her voice. "Try moving now."

Mason Broderick proceeded through what looked like some martial arts kata. He didn't move quite like she'd seen in generic movie montages, but when he was done, he nodded.

"Better. But I think we can fine tune it a bit more. There's still a lag, and the hydraulics aren't compensating enough for the weight difference."

"It's also lacking the torso, which will smooth things out." Victoria folded her arms. Her phone vibrated for the fifth time that hour. *Something must be wrong.* Her lip twitched. Bill could just be fretting over something silly, like one of the boys misplacing something. She wished her voice didn't waver as she continued, "Weight has to be evenly distributed over the body. The arms and legs are designed to work with the strength enhancement of the torso to balance everything."

Broderick nodded and glanced at her glowing, buzzing hip. "Makes sense. Do you need to get that, Ms. Chattham?"

"Yes, please. Excuse me." Ignoring her boss's amused yet disapproving face, mirrored by the rest of his all-but-clones, she casually retreated to the upstairs women's room and called her husband back.

"I rescheduled our session," came his icy voice. "They

couldn't take us any earlier than four weeks out. If you think you can actually get out of work, of course."

Joder. Their couple's therapy had been today. She had missed one for the interview, then missed another. This would be the third reschedule. "I'm sorry, baby. We started testing today and I couldn't get out—"

"Couldn't even answer the phone for two hours?"

"*No,* I *couldn't.*"

"What if it was an emergency?"

"I programmed Krissy's line into your phone for that. Under 'Emergency.'"

"What if I forgot?"

The question hung in the air.

"It wasn't though," she finally said. "And I said I was sorry. I'll *be* at the next meeting. I promise!"

"Yeah, whatever. Enjoy work." The sarcasm in his voice cut.

Victoria heard the click as he slid his phone shut, hard, ending the call. Thank God she was gripping her phone in her flesh hand; her prosthetic one would have crushed the damned thing. With a conscious thought for each flexing muscle, like when she was learning to control the prosthetic, she moved her hand to her pocket and inserted the phone—before she threw it across the bathroom and broke it.

★★★

Only the kitchen lights were on when Victoria pulled into the driveway. Swallowing bitter bile, Victoria ascended the side porch stairs, each feeling higher than normal, and came into the warm kitchen. She picked up the faint smell of chamomile flowers even before she saw Bill at the stove, hand clenched around the tea kettle handle, squinting at the laminated yellow sheet on which the boys had drawn a steaming kettle (different from the steaming coffee-cup-

adorned sheet by the coffee pot) in the corner to help
Daddy keep track of different recipes and kitchen tasks.

What was there to say?

After he set the kettle down, counting five checks that
it was on the burner that he'd ignited, Bill leaned on the
handle of the oven.

Laying her head on his back, she wrapped her arms
around him. "I'm sorry I missed our meeting today."

He didn't say anything, but he didn't push her away.
When the kettle whistled, she let him pour into the two
cups he'd prepared with tea bags. They sat in their usual
seats at the table, kitty-corner from each other where each
could face a kid or reach another kid.

"I miss you." Bill's comment shattered the tangible
silence into slicing shards.

Victoria felt herself deflate. "It's testing. You *know* how
my schedule is for testing. It's my *job.*"

"I *don't* mean…" He stopped and scrunched his face.
"Vic, is this what you want? *This* job I mean. Yes, the
money's good…but are you happy?"

With her eyes closed, Victoria could hear unasked
questions, though she couldn't honestly say she wasn't
hearing her own fears. *Is this job more important than our
marriage? Than our family?*

There was also what she hadn't told Bill. She'd intended
to, but every time she considered it, she'd been afraid to
ruin his good spirits or hadn't wanted to further stress him
when he was already stressed or in pain. Broderick knew
something about her arm. And her abilities. With his
lawyers, if he went to claim her arm, claim every penny of
their savings, their house…she didn't know if she could stop
him.

Was she happy? She loved the project, yes, but *could*
she even quit now if she wasn't? Would Broderick come

after her for whatever secrets he thought she knew to make her arm, and his suit, work? Would he go after her family?

"I don't want to leave my job," she said. At least that was truth. "I'll make things work. I won't miss our next session…I'll black it out on the calendar, set five different alarms on my phone, my email, everything. And I'll find a way to start cutting hours."

Bill stared at her for a long time. He had the most beautiful and intense blue eyes, and they could cut like diamonds. She didn't want to feel she had to hide pieces of her soul from his scrutiny.

She reached across the table and took his hand. "Baby, I just need you to trust me to fix things right now. Please? I need you to trust me."

He snatched his hand back. "Do you know what that *sounds* like?"

She cocked her head, not understanding what *he* thought it sounded like. "Huh?" Then it dawned on her. Late nights, grouchiness, missing family meetings, secrets… Shit! "Oh, God, babe, no-*no!* I…wouldn't even think!"

He snerked, clicking his cup down on the table and pressing his hand over his mouth, possibly holding in tea. After a swallow, he all but giggled. "Obviously not. I can't remember the last time I ever saw you that confused."

"Every guy I work with is an *asshole!*" was all she could sputter.

Bill raised his hands in surrender. "And you *want* to work there?"

"The project we're working on…Broderick bought out Medical Endeavors." She held up her right arm. "It's based on what I did with this…It *means* something to me."

"You never told me that."

"Non-disclosure agreement…Like fifty pages long. I shouldn't have even said this much." She begged him with her eyes to understand.

Taking and releasing a deep breath, Bill nodded and sipped his tea.

***

Mason Broderick resembled a demon when he was not happy, but Victoria stared him down anyway.

"We are on schedule, and I *cannot* miss this appointment. I have had it marked on every calendar in this office for a month now."

"And we've had our testing schedule for two months. You helped put it together." His voice was a cold knife; he didn't even look up from shuffling papers.

"Nowhere in that schedule does it state that we would work eighteen hour days, *every day,* for *all* of testing, with absolutely no personal time, no matter how far ahead we schedule it." Victoria put her hands on her hips and glared harder, hoping to pry his eyes to hers through sheer will.

"It's *your* design that won't work when you're not around." He glanced at her, then back at the papers, the few lines on his face hard as granite. "One might think you're trying to find a way to secure yourself on this project. Especially after I've dropped Miskal, Kerrigan, and Hendricks."

"They were dead weight, and Miskal was smoking pot in storage. We spent more time fixing their screw-ups, so no, I'm not trying to secure my way on this project. I *know* I'm better than anyone on this team. And so do you."

Now he looked up. His eyes were coffee brown, like teddy bear eyes if they weren't so damned cold, a sharp contrast to the fine blond hair gelled perfectly atop his head and neatly groomed over his upper lip. Victoria refused to look away.

The desk phone vibrated Krissy's signature ring. Broderick clenched his jaw. When the phone buzzed again, he gave an almost-inhuman snarl.

"The torso attachments for the arms and legs better be perfect when I try it on tomorrow." He snatched the phone. "What is it?"

Not bothering to hide her smile—she'd take her victories where she could get them—Victoria exited Broderick's office. As she passed Krissy, she heard, "I'm sorry, Mr. Broderick, really. He said he was an attorney, and he swore it was important, and now the line's dead."

Victoria caught her eye and the slightest of winks.

She'd get those damned couplings to work when she got back from her appointment.

★★★

It was nearly ten o'clock at night when Victoria admitted the damned couplings would not be perfect in the morning. Everyone else, even Broderick, had left for the night. It took twenty minutes of a frustrated pace, fighting tears, before a fix came to her. The fix would cost more, but it would work. And it was a reasonable issue—well, reasonable to humans with souls, something she was unsure applied to Broderick—so work could continue on the project without much of a blip. She just needed a certain material…She had better write a proper proposal while she was thinking of it.

Her cell buzzed on her desk. It was Bill. "R U ok?" She puzzled at the message before noticing the time.

Shit. *Joder.* Goddamnit! *Hijo de Dios!*

"Yes. Sorry. Leaving in fifteen."

She finished the proposal in exactly fifteen minutes and promised herself she would go in early to double check it.

★★★

Victoria did not go in early to double check her proposal. Mike woke up with a fever of 102 and Petey's ears hurt. They wanted Mommy.

She appreciated Bill's silence. He was holding back; she knew he wanted to say if she had been back last night, this wouldn't be a surprise for her. Then again, he'd walked in on her sobbing on the downstairs toilet.

"I'll call your sister. She can drive us to the ER." His voice was a mix of emotions she couldn't pick apart as he closed the door.

Broderick was going to fire her. No, worse, he was going to use whatever he knew about the fudged and "misplaced" forms around her prosthetic arm and sue the shit out of her because there was no way her family could afford any lawyer to go up against him. He'd *own* her.

She heard her sister's car arrive and leave the driveway with Bill and the boys. After they drove off, she lifted her head and let out a howl that ended in a stream of curses in three different languages that would be the pride or shame of anyone.

The goddamned mech suit wasn't going to work. It would never work. Like her arm, it only responded to her, to *her* talents, to her...*power* or whatever the hell it was. Victoria had pondered many times on the ability that had manifested in her teens. Her sister, Vivian, had her own gifts, too...charming people, getting them to do things. Victoria could use that right now. Charm Broderick into... well, into not being a dick.

Still on the toilet, trousers and underwear around her ankles, Victoria blew her nose into sheets of toilet paper until she could finally breathe. Vivian had once said that she didn't use her power nearly as much as one would think; the trick was knowing what someone wanted and showing them how helping you got them there.

Broderick had handpicked their whole engineering team, signed them all to secrecy, placed them above every other employee at BWE in paygrade and attention—gave them offices in his *personal building*. She knew this. She also knew that everyone let go still got a ridiculous layoff payment. Every piece of this project had been funded from Mason Broderick's personal accounts, not the business accounts.

Hell, it was a super robot suit. Of course the man wanted it more than anything.

And she *was* the only one who could make it work.

Taking a deep breath, Victoria cleaned herself up, reapplied makeup, and drove into work.

***

"So you decided to come in for testing, after all?"

The men around Mason Broderick turned angry eyes on Victoria. Galliston, next in line for Chief Mechanical Engineer, harrumphed and turned back to the suit, trying to shove the right arm into the socket.

"It's not going to work with brute force. Or did we forget we're all homo sapiens and can actually think?" Her voice was cool, and she stood straight, as if she were taller than every single one of them.

"Then why don't you demonstrate how you fixed the coupling problem *last night*? Or do I need to look deeper into your work with Medical Endeavors to see if I missed anything?" Broderick looked from her eyes to her arm, threat clear.

So this is it.

Victoria strode over to her boss. Eyes wide, as if looking at an oncoming tiger, Galliston moved from her path. She placed her hands on the arms of the suit, then slid them onto the shoulders. It took a millisecond for her to coax the joints to attach to the torso. With her determination, she felt her power extending past what she touched. Even as she moved her hands from the suit, she could manipulate the energy.

This close, she could see the pulse jumping in his neck. Its pattern didn't match what she was picking up from the suit's readings. She frowned. The slight interference she'd picked up when he wore just the arm and leg armor felt stronger, more enhanced. It didn't make sense. The circuit was complete. Victoria knew every tiny part of this suit. There shouldn't *be* any signal she didn't recognize.

He was masking ragged breathing. She smelled cold sweat.

"Mr. Broderick…" Something was *definitely* wrong.

He stepped away from her. Surprise momentarily dissipated the fury and pain as he moved effortlessly.

"Now, show us all how you made this work," he said. "It needs to be replicated. I don't want to need *you* every time I want to use this suit."

Victoria lifted her chin in defiance. "No."

"*What?*"

"I have worked my ass off more than Any. One. Else. on this team, including *you*, and you don't want to *need* me?"

He narrowed his eyes, but she noticed the day-bright overhead LEDs reflecting a sheen of sweat down his cheeks and neck.

"Have one of them get you out of that contraption." Victoria gestured dismissively at the suit. "And then tell me you don't want to *need* me. In the meantime, I have a proposal to rewrite so we can fix some of the problems the *team* will eventually find if they can work half as hard as I do." She turned on her heel, strode out of the testing area, and took the stairs back up to the offices.

Krissy was frowning on the phone, obviously on an intense personal call. Using the distraction to her advantage, Victoria walked past her own office, where her proposal lay in the middle of the desk.

She needed to know exactly *what* Mason Broderick had on her. How much was he bluffing, and how much of a case *could* he take against her and her arm?

With said arm, it didn't take much effort to break the lock on his office door.

She glanced around the sparse office. It was almost clinical, it was so clean. Five different sets of black file cabinets, unmarred by the least dust mote, shone in sunlight streaming through the wall of windows. Pursing her lips, she regarded his desk where a sloppy pile of mail, likely left by Krissy, rebelled against the pristine order.

One envelope was placed atop the others, and Victoria recognized the medical company's logo immediately.

They only made and patented one specific item: high-end pacemakers.

"The dude really is like Tony Stark." This certainly explained the unexpected feedback she'd sensed.

This changed everything.

Inhumanly heavy footfalls thundered from the stairs.

"Mason?!" she heard Krissy scream.

As she'd designed it, the suit moved faster than humanly possible. Broderick shoved the door open so hard it cracked against the wall, bouncing to slam shut behind him. Thoroughly drenched in sweat, face twisted in pain, he approached.

She ought to be terrified at the armored human before her. Even without weapons, the strength in the limbs, alone, could crush every bone in her body.

Victoria folded her arms and smiled.

"Get. This. Goddamned. Thing. Offa-me!" His voice betrayed the pain.

"You're experiencing myocardial infarction," she stated. "Brilliant as you are otherwise, you're an idiot. Did you think this huge magnetic machine set to your vitals wouldn't mess with your pacemaker?"

"I had...it...specially...made. It wasn't...Just. Take. This. Off!" His metal hand clutched his metal chest.

"See, I take it off, your heart stops. You don't want that, do you?" There was more than a twinge of guilt as she saw his suffering. But still. Things could not go back to how they were. She would not lose this contract. And she could not risk him destroying her family with his lawyers.

"You can. Restart it."

"Here's where I chose whether to play innocent and not know *what* you're talking about, or I can just cut to the chase because I was sick of these games when you started playing them." She paused for effect. "Yeah, I can restart it. And I can stop it again. And I can fix it so your mechanical ticker plays nice with your mechanical armor for the rest of your life."

"What...do you...want?"

"Glad you're with me on the 'done playing games' part." She walked up to him, and pressed her left hand to the armor chest. "I want...this arm." Victoria held up her right arm. "Mine. Period. No strings attached. And I want this contract." She tapped her forefinger on his chest. "Also mine, all mine. I'll even be nice and ask for the salary of only half the team combined. Saves you money for the improvements I can make on this." She tapped his metal suit again. "*I* can make this thing work, and *I* can keep it running, and *I* can keep your ticker issues secret...because that's the only reason I can see you being stupid enough not to let us know about it.

"Last, and not least, starting right now, my family comes first and don't you *ever* forget that. You take care of them and let me enjoy my life with them, I'll return the favor. Go save the world, rule the world, I really don't care, but me and mine get taken care of. Am I clear?"

He paused. She wasn't sure if it was for effect, to maintain whatever dignity he felt he had left, or if it was the pain overcoming him. Finally, he nodded. "Clear. Deal."

"Good." Victoria pressed the flat of her left hand to his chest. With the help of her robotic hand, she eased him to the ground as the suit clanked to the floor around him, no longer holding him up. He curled up as the rest of the armor released. She pressed her left hand to his chest, searching for the signal of the pacemaker. He convulsed once, but she held him steady, resetting the charges to his heart.

As soon as she felt it regulate, she stepped away from him. It did not escape her notice that she still felt the energy, like a slight buzz in the palm of her hand. One more step back made it weaken, but not fade entirely.

He lay on the floor for several minutes, just breathing. As he sat up, he looked at her. The curiosity in his eyes tempered his threat. "I could have you arrested."

"You're not going to, though."

He regarded her a few more minutes. Half naked, covered in sweat, shorter and younger than Victoria, he didn't lose his imposing air. She didn't flinch.

"One addendum."

"Mmn?"

"You don't care if I'm saving the world or ruling it so long as your family is okay. Fine, then don't ask. No questions about where I'm going, what I'm doing, who I'm with. Nothing. No prying, peeking…or the deal's off. Am I clear?"

Victoria took her time considering. It didn't require the time, but she was getting the hang of the power of the pause. "Clear. And agreed."

"Good. Then, before you leave, at five, I want a draft of the contract delivered to me, personally along with your proposal for improvements based on today's test."

"I'll have both done by four, at which time I'm taking a whole hour of the accumulated PTO from the past four months and going home."

"Past hours do *not* get figured into your new paid time off schedule."

Victoria tensed her mouth. She wasn't budging. Not this far into things.

"You can leave any time today once both the contract and proposal are in my hands. We start counting accumulated PTO tomorrow, when you'll still arrive at promptly nine a.m."

She considered. It was a compromise, but one she felt comfortable making. "All right. I will see you when I deliver the contract and the proposal. And again at nine nine a.m."

At his nod, she turned to leave, then paused. The connection to his pacemaker—she could identify it now—barely tingled her palm. Turning once more, she smiled. "Also, so you don't think your lawyers can work me over later..." She closed the fist of her flesh hand and watched him clutch his chest. "From anywhere. Good day, Mr. Broderick." Opening her hand, she turned to go, leaving him sitting amid a mess of robot armor parts. He didn't have to know that she was just discovering her range.

Tonight, she would cook Bill dinner and make him tea. And then she would definitely tuck in her boys. And maybe break out her dad's old comic collection.

HER EYES HOLD THE SECRETS
OF THE OCEAN AND THE MOON

I first saw her in rusty, copper silhouette
as the dying day bled red upon the world.
She danced upon the wet rocks
in torn jeans, T-Shirt, and tattered flannel
that in that light flittered like a Gothic nightgown—
like a maiden welcoming her sacrifice
to the sea.
I came when she beckoned,
though far less sure-footed than she
on frothing slime and shifting stones
forever surrendering themselves
to the sea.

When I was close enough
or perhaps the sun had died enough,
I could see her face.
Her wild smile promised pleasure
only found in dangerous waters.

Her eyes were the shifting void
of blues and greys and greens
of the element stretched before us.

She invited me to dance.
I wanted to, but was afraid to fall.

"Then feed me your fear," she said,
and then she kissed me.
I let her swallow my fear.
I danced with her on the rocks
until the moon rose, rusty and copper,
still stained with the day's death.
Then she danced with me
as I invited her to my bed.

We most often go to beaches,
the rocky ones; she holds sand in contempt.
"It's soft and broken, too gentle for my taste."
I am a gentle person at heart;
I fear she will learn this and leave me,
broken and soft, in her wake.
She tells me, "The rocks are always wet,
waiting and welcoming the violent tides."
I don't miss her meaning;
I make myself as fierce as waxing moon waves
and make love to her on the rocks.

Her eyes are the glimmering trick
of green water upon green stones,
the slick slip indiscernible from solid step.

On full moons, we sit on the rocks in flagrant defiance
of Police Take Notice signs.
I am sure she allows only whom she wants
to take notice of her presence.
The rising moon lends its glow to her skin
as it does to the waves—
sometimes golden, sometimes blood rust
always haunted by more time than
humans can conceive.

As the moon rises,
shrinking and paling amongst countless stars,
I break off pieces of myself and feed them to her.
Her dewy lips caress my fingers;
her shark-sharp teeth gnaw my being.
Her rise and fall teach pleasure found only
in the space between the most primal fears.

"Some people claim the ocean brings them peace,"
she says
as she lays upon
the quivering flesh of what's left of me.
"And what of it?" I ask. I know I must challenge her.
To just listen would reveal my gentleness; she may leave
and break my heart into a million grains of sand.
"The ocean is a merciless deity that creates and destroys.
It is what it is."
I ponder, "Some people call the ocean the Mother of Life."
"It is. The best mothers are merciless."
I roll us over with a wave, so I am atop her on the rocks.
"And what do you know of motherhood, my love?"
She says nothing, but smiles and looks at me
as if I should know that answer,
and I do.

Her eyes are the swirl of countless salty tears,
water broken from the wombs of worlds,
and the ocean that births and consumes its dead.

I'm prepared to feed her the last of me
that I may always be with her.
I follow her down to the overlap of
of waiting wet rocks and devouring waves
on bare feet nearly as sure-stepping as hers.

I have grown good at pretending
sharp stones and barnacle bites don't bother me,
that I don't see the bloody footprints
I leave behind.
It occurs to me I have loved this woman
for a full year and have never seen her bleed.
It occurs to me it has also been some time
since I've seen my blood—
besides footprints licked clean by the waves.
She pushes me to the rocks
with the strength of the sea,
and I open myself for her to feed.
I swell, carried on waves of pleasure,
as she consumes me with kisses,
swallowing the ocean I give—
the ocean drawn from me by her touch.

Her eyes are flickering silver fishes,
churning toward suffocating air
to escape the rising whale's maw.

The way I lie on the rocks,
the way she looms above me,
lit by the sunken-sunstained sky,
both our bellies bloat with pregnancy,
life and mystery, blood and sacred offering.
I arch toward her hungry mouth;
consumed by a hungry wave, my failing is found.

My gentleness flees from hiding; it screams primal fear.
It trespasses upon my ecstasy, poisons my sacrificial bliss.
As each rise toward culmination recedes,
the watery loss of *me* fills its place.
I am stricken with realization; I scream primal fear.

With the ebb of terror flows delicious desire.
I am at war with myself—
Surrender or death is the gentle option.

Her eyes are the storms that unmake worlds,
that smash dreams and bodies upon rocks
beneath unspeakably beautiful, eternal waters.

The moon rises high enough for me to see it
between the blinding waves that steal my breath.
The moon is her face and her eyes,
and in that moment, I understand
the entirety of the ocean—
It is merciless, yes, and omnipotent.
It is also everything else.
Like all humans who dare love something immortal,
my being is unmade by unfathomable eternity.
I am a temporary diversion
from the numbing effects of timelessness
and endlessness.
I would always be too gentle for the likes of her.
My heart breaks, smashed into a million grains of sand
and I flow from her embrace with the pull of waves.
For just a moment—

Her eyes are stilled waves after the storm,
the quiet mourning of unseen depths of loss,
an unbroken reflection of the heavens.

For just a moment, the ocean pauses.
But the ocean is what it is—
or so I briefly knew—
and standing still for more than a moment,
mourning one loss for more than a moment,

would unmake everything else.

Her eyes are the maddening, shattered light
of an unreachable,
ever-moving boundary between elements,
and the darkness that cradles all life and death.

GARDENS OF NEW
BUBASTIS

GARDENS OF NEW BUBASTIS

Doctor Shadia Obast was not the first veterinary geneticist to create a designer genmod cat that could talk, but she did create the most famous one.

The Egyptian Coon cat Pharoahess Hatshepsut Americaine Sacred Smoke, as she was known in the international show circuits, had been recorded as making almost two thousand distinct vocalizations, which was at the level of some of the smartest domestic or captive birds on record. The breed, which could only include genetic material from purebred Maine Coons, sphynx cats, and Siamese, was also not Obast's design. But she was credited with its perfection.

"Smokey," as her humans Ambré and Hernane addressed her, was the star of her breed. She showcased both the desired intelligence and the beauty genmod-breeders should strive for. Or, rather, she showcased the beauty and intelligence the designer veterinary geneticists contracted by licensed breeders should strive for.

Smokey was also a spoiled-rotten princess that, unbeknownst to the show audiences and the last batch of breed auditors, needed daily hormone therapy shots to preserve the luxurious, eight-inch-long ear tufts, feline fetlocks, and tail—the only parts of her wrinkly, grey body that grew fur. The little beast also needed a special diet that included regular calming herbs for her "irrepressible" personality.

Like most highly intelligent companion animals, if not

regularly stimulated, Smokey would systematically destroy anything she got her hairless paws and sharp claws into. Obast had tried to warn the couple about this trait when she was designing the litter of embryos, but sometimes humans listened worse than cats *not* genmodded for linguistic capabilities. Her lectures fell on deaf ears, and unfortunately, Ambré was unprepared to find her favorite pair of Christian Louboutins shredded to lacy threads hanging from blood-red soles. The foolish woman had left them out in the room where she'd locked the cat during yet another dinner party. This one included a Parisian couple whose geneticist had created a hypoallergenic Siberian Bengal-Rex so the wife could enjoy a cat the husband could show at the Top Tier Experimental GenMod Showcase.

"Rreet, rreet. Rnow, rreet. Rnow, rnow, rheet," was the current vocabulary Smokey was demonstrating to Obast while trying to create the most elaborate tripping pattern around the geneticist's calves as she prepared today's hormone serum.

"You'll get your treats soon. Not now, but soon," Obast cooed to her "baby" as she tried to surreptitiously fill the syringe to the proper dosage.

Obast had done the genetic treatments that created her first successful show cat. She'd overseen the development of the litter of embryos and had nursed the kittens who'd survived "birth" from the incubators. She'd affectionately dubbed this one the "Smoke Beast" for the silvery reverse points on her ears, feet, and tail that contrasted to the dark grey of her hairless body—as well as for her domineering personality and destructive tendencies upon boredom and displeasure.

Being happy with Obast's contracted creation, Ambré and Hernane had incorporated the nickname into her show name, which was derived from the genetic material—or feline "breeding lines"—as required of all genmod cats. Despite the mountains of documentation Dr. Obast submitted with each attempted animal in each attempted litter, The International Genmod Cat Association, as well as the Federal Department of Genetic Modification, required each show cat be genetically identifiable based on name.

Strangely enough, at least to Obast, once the designer cat had been cleared to go to her home, all documentation went through the "breeders." The veterinary geneticist had always been required to send official copies of the paperwork to the couple who'd contracted her; now Ambré and Hernane were responsible for receiving all documentation and forwarding it to the IGCA and the FDGM. This small change of priorities left enough of a window to bury the reporting of the hormone injections.

The Smoke Beast, as with all the veterinary geneticist's patients, was supposed to be kept in her kennel during lab visits as regulation code stated. Obast, however, felt it was more in the spirit of the code—which was written "to ensure an atmosphere of utmost safety, security, and humane treatment for the permitted breeding population of professional felines"—to give her cats a chance to exercise and explore. Knowing the dangers a lab presented to at-liberty animals, Obast took extra measures to keep her lab clean, organized, and cat-proofed.

Inasmuch as one can keep any location "cat-proofed."

Luckily, there hadn't been an incident in years. And Obast's (or rather, Ambré's and Hernane's) reputation in the breeding community, along with her high scores from the genmod auditors, meant she'd not been mandated to have a live feed camera anywhere besides her receiving area, pharmaceutical storage, and in-use embryonic labs and incubators.

As with other exceptionally smart animals, Smokey

paid close attention to the world around her and could make specific associations. While Obast did her best to create as many positive associations with her lab as possible —it was where her patients got treats, got lots of pets, got playful stimuli—it didn't change that it was also where many would get unpleasant treatments. And nearly all of Obast's clients knew what a shot looked like.

Obast had prepared for that.

Upon spying the injector, the Smoke Beast hissed out a word that sounded a lot like "bitch" and darted to a thin, dark opening between Obast's shelves and the wall. With a chuckle, the doctor flipped a switch on the inside panel of the bookcase and a soft hiss-*schick* locked the hidden cage.

"Ucking hitch-hitch, asshkole ucker…"

Obast could not recall having heard some of these particular vocalizations Smokey was sharing on the live-recorded tests during the intellect portion of shows. Biting her lip to keep from laughing out loud, she imagined Ambré and Hernane debating encouragement of vulgarity. While a couple of their social standing wouldn't want to be associated with such vocabulary, these utterances were still potential words they could claim the animal knew—points solidifying Smokey's status as the star model of her breed.

That status, and the income and reputation associated with it, had allowed Obast to open her own clinic that specialized in designer cats. More importantly, it paid for her studies of genetic diseases in non-genmod cats and let her take on a few pro bono cases for cats and families who needed her specialized knowledge. Additionally, in her private apartment that she'd built on top of her lab, she personally cared for the cats she'd created that had survived genmod "birth" but were not star models. The ones that didn't deserve to be handed over to the processors with other unwanted felines. Despite the laws mandating such.

Those criminal contraband babies would get her love and attention when she returned home. For now, she continued to croon at the cussing-her-out fancy cat and manipulated the squeeze-box carrier to expose the hairless flesh of the Smoke Beast's shoulder for the injection. If nothing else, the designed hair pattern made it easier to give the poor girl her many shots. Upon release, Smokey gave a confused shake and trotted over to the food. After chittering excitedly, she tucked her fluffy feet under her grey, wrinkly torso, and delicately ate in tiny bites.

When the cat finished eating—quicker than her etiquette would have suggested—Obast kissed the silky strands of fur between the cat's flowing-tuft ears and scritched her fingers against the prickly wrinkles around Smokey's neck.

With a purr-rasping chitter, the Smoke Beast dove for the shiny styli in Obast's lab coat, demanding her full attention. Pinching one stylus up from the pocket, the doctor let the cat "catch" the shiny stick. The Beast batted it around the desk, pausing to chitter, stalk, and possibly call the captured writing utensil a *"hitch-hitch-hitch-hitch-ucking-hitch."* Obast's belly laugh evoked a most offended glare from Smokey's sharp blue eyes. Primly dropping the pen, the cat sauntered to the far side of the desk, her back to the human, and began bathing with long, luxurious licks.

"You are quite the princess, aren't you?" Obast asked with another chuckle.

"Rinsiss," came from the cat, who glanced between the treat cabinet and the human. When no treat was forthcoming, she tried again. *"Kreffer."*

"Are you saying you're a clever girl?" Obast responded, getting out the fancy, cushioned travel box that had brought Smokey to the lab.

"Hess. Kreffer kurl."

Obast imagined Ambré, who was always the show handler, practicing this exact script for hours.

Smiling with the same pride as her mother had done upon Obast's second doctoral graduation, the geneticist said, "Well, I suppose you are. How about some treats if you go to bed?"

"*Rreet.*"

The look on the cat's face and the declarative tone of her vocalization made Obast question how much of these "words" were mimicry or trained tricks...and how much comprehension there might actually be.

She folded her arms and looked at the cat as one would look at a child who'd just learned they could sass. The cat returned to her bath. Obast went to the treat cabinet, an action that garnered full feline attention and a seductive chitter, and placed the tiny green fish chew directly in front of the carrier. "Bed."

Smokey stared a moment, then offered another purring chitter, rolling onto her back. If Obast were one to anthropomorphize more, she'd translate the communication as, *Why don't you just bring that treat over here, dear human?*

But she was a doctor of science and medicine. And she knew the cat understood commands. Tapping her finger next to the treat, she repeated, "Bed."

With a great yawn and stretch, the cat jumped from the desk, sashayed to the examination table—ear tufts, leg fur, and nearly two-foot-long tail fluttering in her stride—and hopped in front of the carrier. Settling just outside the door, she nibbled the offering and chirped, "*Rreet,*" once again.

"Get in bed and *then* you get another." Obast gestured into the carrier.

After yet another cartoonishly long yawn and stretch, the *model star* slllooowwly stepped each paw into the crate and turned around. "*Rreet.*"

Sputtering one more laugh, Obast pulled out another treat from the bag, declaring. "You are lucky you're so cute. You know that?"

"*Hyoot,*" muttered Smokey, graciously taking the treat out of Obast's hand.

Shaking her head, Obast grabbed the carrier and headed to the plush waiting area where one of Smokey's humans should have just arrived.

★★★

It was close to midnight when Obast secured Parti, the most recent addition to her secret family, into her kennel. Parti was the only survivor of the recent Bengalese Rex litter Hernane had requested, in hopes of getting a hypoallergenic cat with mid-length, velvety fur in the unique patterns of Bengals. Something even *nicer* than what the Parisian couple had, if possible. Not that they were being competitive about it. It was all for the genetic studies, Obast told herself.

Unfortunately for Parti, while her dander measured as low as her Balinese ancestors, her coat was short and hardly distinguishable from a brawny, non-genmod calico tabby. Her genetic material was solid and usable—collected and frozen during the mandatory spay for any genmod cats with functioning sexual organs—but Parti, herself, was not a star model. She clung to Obast upon being returned to her kennel, but kept her claws mostly retracted and gave the most pitiful multisyllabic vocalization that resembled one of those sad sheepherder yodels. Personality and unique vocalizations were just not enough in today's genmod cat world.

Obast gave her an extra treat, sighing about the strict provisions that didn't allow genmod cats to be homed outside of licensed breeders, entertainers, show-families, or laboratory facilities. Any unwanted "product" was sent to processors who logged the genetic material—including the required geneticist-creator's signature code on the X chromosomes—and declared it safe or unsafe for consumption. Unsafe product was incinerated, destroying any potentially hazardous genetic material.

When Obast had learned this fact in grade school, long before she'd traded her parents' name-address for her vocational name-address, she'd decided then and there to never eat meat or anything processed—and to begin volunteering at cat shelters, working to find animals homes before they were killed.

Taking a few moments to pet all nine of the cats she'd falsely declared dead, she sent a small prayer to the ancient goddess Bast, from whom she took her name and the name of her facility. She didn't worship the goddess, exactly...she didn't worship much of anything. But she'd always felt a connection to cats since a feral one followed her home on her very first day of school. She'd sworn to do a massive list of chores—and all her brother's chores—so long as she could keep it. She'd kept that oath. And she never once complained about the work.

Not all of her "babies" were as robust as Parti, and more than thrice their number had not survived past their first few months after "birth." Some she'd secretly euthanized because of apparent pain; others had died on their own. In a hidden freezer were carefully wrapped members of the latter fate.

When she visited her family on Friday, they would be transferred into the gardens where they'd feel love once more—for eternity.

***

Pharoahess Nefertiti Yang Liryadel, a Teacup Aby-Singapurr, dominated the Kitten categories of the New York

New Breed Expo. Obast even received her first show award —complete with a cash prize—for being the breed creator. Ambré and Hernane were delighted with the second addition to their family, affectionately nicknamed "TeeLee." At barely a pound, the tiny cat would always look like a kitten, had silken blue seal point fur, and was already demonstrating almost twelve hundred vocalizations.

Two days after returning from the show, Ambré juggled two hissing, yowling, (and cussing) fancy carriers into Obast's clinic without an appointment. "Please, Shadia, dear, Hernane and I are at our wits' end!"

The desperation on the woman's face was enough to soften the hearts of the other humans, who nodded their acceptance of waiting a little longer.

Obast took the larger of the two cat carriers from Ambré, knowing she could better handle eleven pounds of the thrashing Smoke Beast, and led the way to the examination room. She cooed softly, feeling the cat calm and hearing her muttering move from hissing "*ucking-hitch-hitch*" to whining demands for "*reets*", "*hrets,*" and "*suggle-ee.*"

Ambré put TeeLee's carrier on the table first, which meant that Obast couldn't immediately administer the pets and snuggles Smokey was crying for. Obast did pause as she put the larger cat's carrier down, making a few more soothing kissy noises until the cat's volume dropped just a little more and she lay down, facing away and smacking her massive tail side to side to show her intense displeasure.

Obast gently extricated the tiny kitten from the carrier, grimacing as she saw the bloody gashes and torn ear.

"Is she going to be all right?" Ambré bent close to the cage, her worried face tight with grief.

Obast was already checking vitals and looking closely at the wounds. "I'm sure she will. I have some medical glue that should close these without leaving any scars. So, what happened?"

"I don't know," Ambré said, a sob to her voice. "I mean, I just let TeeLee out of her room to be with Smokey and Smokey dove at her. Yesterday it happened too, but I thought it was just the stress from being in the show…"

"Have you been introducing them slowly?"

"Yes. They were getting along fine before the show. I mean, they didn't really spend a lot of time with each other, and TeeLee is just such a love bug that she stays on our laps or in our pockets…"

Obast tensed, suspecting what the problem could be. "Have you, not meaning to of course, been giving TeeLee more attention than Smokey?" With a gentle swiftness, she gave the cat a tiny shot of tranquilizer and anesthetic.

"Do cats get jealous like that?"

Of course they do! Obast wanted to scold, but she kept her voice calm. "Oh yes, especially ones as intelligent as Smokey and TeeLee. You want to make sure you still give them both the same attention," she explained as she cleaned all the wounds.

"I didn't think…I mean, we love them both. Just, TeeLee is so tiny and this was her first show…"

Obast patiently sealed the wounds as she offered several ways Ambré and Hernane could ensure both cats felt loved—as well as what to watch for as warnings that the cats were not getting along. Ambré nodded, repeating most of it back to Obast's approval, but she continued to cuddle little TeeLee as the doctor inspected Smokey.

"Why don't you tuck her away and remind Smokey you love her, too?" the doctor prodded when she finished sealing the tiny scratches on the larger cat.

"Oh yes, of course." Ambré did so, but Obast sensed a nervousness in the woman…and noticed a few splashes of blood on her cream blouse.

"Did you get scratched breaking them up?" she asked.

"Well, yes...but it's nothing really..."

"Let me see," Obast said, gently picking up Smokey, kissing her, and placing her in her carrier with several treats. "I'm fairly adept at human first aid, too."

Ambré chuckled, crossing her arms and leaning in a pose Obast would call "demure," if not a little flirty, based on the few films she'd seen. Obast folded her arms and raised her eyebrow in the "Come on. Be an adult, now" look her parents had perfected over years of dealing with her and her brother's stubbornness.

Biting her lip nervously, Ambré slid up her sleeves, offering her the dark arms that were still seeping blood from more scratches than Obast could count. While the doctor cleaned the wounds and applied the sealant, Ambré leaned closer. Uncomfortably so.

When the doctor was done cleaning and bandaging, Ambré stepped into her personal space even more. She brushed her perfectly manicured fingers up Obast's wrist with a "Thank you" that resembled a purr.

Obast felt a hammering in her chest. Having another person outside of her immediate family so close to her was physically distressing. And she wasn't naïve enough, not after years of explanations and teasing from old college friends and her brother...not after what had happened with her advisor...to not recognize what Ambré's posture and actions might be suggesting. The woman's eyes even seemed to grow a little wider and her lips a little poutier.

Besides, this woman was her contracted client—responsible for her greatly expanded bank account.

Obast was unaware of any problems, outside of introducing TeeLee, in Ambré and Hernane's household or relationship. Why would Ambré act this way? Perhaps she was reading this entire thing wrong.

The doctor well knew she was better at reading cats than humans.

Obast quickly stepped away and dumped the bloodied sterilizing pads into the hazmat container. "Those will heal up with no scars on you, either. Is there anything else I can do for the cats right now?" She hoped her question struck the right balance of subtlety and clarity.

Ambré studied her a moment, the look in her topaz eyes resembled that of a cat deciding if it should stalk or not.

In a purely aesthetic sense, Obast knew Ambré was an especially beautiful woman. And one who was used to being appreciated for that beauty. However...well, Obast had no interest outside of their professional relationship and ensuring the cats were well cared for. And while she'd never felt this type of troublesome desire for anyone, the doctor felt even if she had, she would never be so foolish as to complicate her career in such a manner.

"Would you like some help carrying out the cages?" Obast offered, hoping her smile conveyed the professionalism she was striving for. If Ambré took offense, would she take it out on the cats? Would she jeopardize Obast's career? The woman had the money and the power to do that, too. One call from a person of Ambré's status to the IGCA might get Obast blacklisted from contracting with any other genmod breeding families; a call to the FDGM might bar the doctor from any veterinary work whatsoever—or find her a felon if they learned of adjusted records or improperly handled "genetic material."

Ambré simply nodded. "Please. Thank you so much for seeing me on such short notice, Doctor."

Obast picked up Smokey's crate and tried to make her smile even more welcoming—but not so much as to seem like she was sending mixed messages. "You know I'm here for the cats whenever you need. Let me know how things continue."

"Of course. You know, I think I can handle both of them. Good day, Doctor." Ambre took Smokey from Obast's hand, pausing once again as their fingers brushed.

Obast managed to not snatch her hand away, but she felt like she was trying to dart through peanut butter as she went to hold the office door for Ambré's exit. One of her front desk staff—goodness upon her for being so attentive—saw to holding the main doors as Ambré left at a stalk that still befit her class status. An equally observant veterinary assistant took the next human and cat to another exam room, giving her a few minutes.

Obast shut herself in the room she was in and slumped against the door. *What was that? Was it even anything? And if it was, what might go wrong from it?*

One thing could certainly go wrong—if it were discovered Smokey had injured a human, she'd be put down immediately and without mercy.

***

Abraham Adel, Obast's younger brother, scowled at Smokey and removed her from the dining room table for the third time. "And your clients want *you* to have this beast for the weekend because...?" he growled.

"She's not getting along with the newest cat they had me create." Obast caught the cat midleap to her desired location, careful of this latest round of healing scratches and what she hoped was a bruise from falling rather than a human hand or foot. "They're clearly not listening to me on how to introduce them, and that's creating problems. I'm sorry, but she also just hates being alone."

Hoping to compromise with her brother's disapproval of her bringing the cat into the home he and his wife shared with their mother, she placed Smokey between her and her mother. Her mom's eyes lit up as if this was the first time she noticed the cat, even though they'd been there for a few hours. The older woman began to dote to the feline's approval.

"You are such a strange kitty, you are. But you are cute, you are. Who's a cute kitty? Who's a cute kitty?"

Obast gave her brother a look to say "see, it was a good thing I brought a cat even though you hate them" and moved the cat to her mother's lap, explaining who Smokey was for the third time that afternoon.

With a chuff, Abraham retrieved the whistling kettle and poured it into a pot of fresh tea leaves. As if trying to bridge the gap between the siblings, his wife Nebla passed another slice of buttered brown bread and said, "That interview with you the other night looked like it went really well. And it was very sweet of you to tag her genetic line with your parents' names like that."

Obast smiled. She'd held her breath when she'd suggested including Liryadel—a combination of Leary for her mother and Adel for her father—as TeeLee's show name and thus the name passed on to any of her line made with that genetic material. "Well, I couldn't have made it through my first medical degree if they hadn't helped me pay for it. I wanted to honor them in a way that could carry on for generations."

Her brother softened upon hearing that, relaxing more in his chair.

"You see, I still wasn't quite sure what I was doing with Smokey. But I could plan things out better for TeeLee—"

"*Uckinghitch,*" came a snarl from Smokey.

Both Abraham and Obast sat up in case the cat took out her ire upon their wheelchair-bound mother. Abraham gave Obast a "you brought that hell beast into my house" glare, but the cat made no move against the old woman.

For her part, Anita Leary threw her head back and laughed. "It sounded like she said naughty words! Naughty-mouth kitty! Naughty, naughty."

Smokey seemed to appreciate the heavy neck head scritching that came with her new lap's mirth, so she repeated a purring, *"Authy. Authy."*

"You hear that? I had an old beau once who had one of those talking...talking...you know what I mean. Just like that!"

Both Obast and Abraham slouched back in their seats.

"Birds, Ma?" Abraham offered. "Your old beau had a talking bird?"

"Yes, yes, that and that...You know what I mean, Moses." Her pale blue eyes darted back to the cat. "Can you say 'Pretty kitty'? Pretty kitty!"

"I'm Abraham, Ma," he corrected tiredly.

Anita didn't notice, didn't hear, or didn't care as she continued to get the cat to repeat what she said. She laughed at each success. With a resigned chuckle, because their mother was clearly delighted, Abraham poured their tea and regarded his sister. "So, is the Beast the *only* one with injuries, Cat Sister?"

"I...what?" She blinked several times, edging back in her chair and lifting her tea cup between them as if it were some shield from the unexpected probing and concern in his eyes. Not entirely sure what to make of his question, words continued to fumble out of her mouth, "Ambré and Hernane...? They wouldn't raise a hand to me."

Now it was her brother's turn to be taken aback. He narrowed his eyes with even more worry as Nebla asked, "Are you worried your employers are hurting your cats?"

"No, no. I don't believe so...I mean, they do love their cats." She glanced at the blackish bruise across Smokey's haunch. The cat could have fallen in the fight, as Ambré had claimed. Or a human could have kicked her trying to separate her from TeeLee—who was cut up and stressed so badly from Smokey that she couldn't fly out to the Dubai show next week as planned.

"You don't sound nearly so sure of that," Abraham pointed out.

"I *don't* believe they'd deliberately hurt one of their animals, or anyone really. I just…know they are having a tough time with the two cats getting along."

After a pause filled only with their mother still chatting with the cat, Abraham asked, "And how do they feel about the ones you buried in our gardens this afternoon?"

The tea's steam made the heat in Obast's cheeks uncomfortable. "You know they don't know. No one knows," she answered between gritted teeth. "No one *can* know."

"And no one will. But look, Shadi," he said gently. "I don't mean to be difficult, but you haven't been yourself lately."

"Hmph. Well, they say fame changes people. I'm a famous, award-winning designer geneticist now. Of course I'll be different."

"You know that's not what I mean." Abraham put his teacup down. Nebla respectfully turned her attention to Anita while the siblings spoke. "I don't expect you to stop coming over for Saturday tea just because you've doubled what you put into Ma's accounts."

Obast slouched deeper in the chair, resting her teacup on her lips with a scowl.

"You don't think I wouldn't notice that?"

"I paid off all our debts years ago. My family is all of you and my cats. Of course I'm going to look after all of you. I *am* still the oldest."

"I'm not ungrateful, Shadi; I'm not. Even if I get tenure, I'm never going to make in my lifetime what you've made in just a few years. That's not the point." Abraham took a deep breath. "And this isn't me being old-fashioned like dad, either, because I'm the *man* of the family," he added pointedly. "I just *know* you. And I know how many animals you've buried in our back yard, and I *know* when your clothes are loose because you're not eating and when you're looking stressed and pale…and I *know* I'm lucky you remember to call just to let me know you're coming every Saturday."

"I hardly ever miss Saturday tea!" Why was she feeling so defensive from her *little* brother?

"I know. And that means a lot to me, to us…to Mom." Abraham closed his eyes. "But you called 'to chat' once last week and twice this week. You don't chat. You never chat. And you never ask permission to bury animals in the back yard. How many times have you reminded us who paid off the mortgage?"

"I-I only mentioned the mortgage once, maybe twice. And it's only because I want to put them somewhere nice and not have them sent to be processed for food or fertilizer or whatever else. I *know* what I'm creating; they're not messing with the soil or food or flowers or anything."

Obast had researched decomposition, particularly that of genmods, very well. Part of the reason she'd insisted on paying off the mortgage was because her family lived in one of the few single-home neighborhoods left outside of Alexandria, and their land was surrounded by high walls and bushes. The backyard gardens of flowers, vegetables, and herbs had been her mother's pride and joy. Nebla, a trained nurse, regularly said that the ability for her mother to still spend time even just sitting in the gardens had done more than the gene therapy at keeping the ninety-seven-year-old woman's dementia at bay. Abraham claimed it was all the love and prayers their mother had spent nurturing the gardens, and then using the gardens' flowers and fruits to nurture her family—now it was giving back to her.

Obast was well aware of the limitations of genetic therapy to treat mental disorders. And while she refused to anthropomorphize plants, she knew the gardens *were* loved. A lot of tender and nurturing moments had happened in her family's gardens—and a lot still did. To bury a loved one, to care about their final resting place, was an act of love. While her contract with Ambré and Hernane dictated that the animals she created belonged to them, a contract could not dictate the love Obast put into her creations. That was hers alone to give.

"It's not the gardens I worry about," Abraham clarified.

She supposed no contract could give parameters to a brother's love either. There was no agreement prohibiting him from caring about her in a most aggravating manner.

Obast felt her shirt bunching up past her neck and sat herself back up, head high. This—this slouching, defensive mouse was *not* her. No. Narrowing her eyes at her *baby* brother, she said, "Look, I do good work. I take very good care of my family, first and foremost, as our parents taught." She ignored the part about honoring God even before that and continued faster and more emphatic before the more pious Abraham could interject. "And I help people too poor to get specialized medical care for their cats. My work, my studies have developed a cure, *a cure* to feline infectious peritonitis and just about *wiped out* polycystic kidney disease. The genetic therapies being tried out for rabies immunity will help *many* animals, including humans. Those treatments came from *my* research. I know there's a cost, and I do my best to give all my creations as much joy as I can. And while I'm not exactly a fan of entitled rich bitches running designer cat shows, their money is funding everything I do!"

"*Hitch-hitch-hitchess,*" Smokey said gleefully, rolling around on Anita's lap, clawlessly batting at the limp hands above her.

Anita, however, looked between the two siblings, eyes wide. "What's wrong? What's wrong?"

"It's all right, Anita." Nebla rubbed the woman's arms and guided her hand back to the cat. "Did you see the kitty who came to see you today?"

"What an odd cat! It looks just like one of those fancy poodles with its haircut. But you're still so cute…"

"*Cyoo. Cyoot.*"

Abraham gestured with his head to the kitchen as Nebla and Smokey continued to sooth their mother. Obast followed.

"You *are* upset," he said. After a pause, he asked, "Is it about your boss maybe hitting on you?"

Her gaze shot to his eyes.

"Did you think I wasn't listening when you called?"

Had she told him on the phone? She didn't remember. She remembered rambling, perhaps. "No! And no." That was a lie. On both of his questions. "And they are my *clients*, not my bosses." She could clear that up, at least. Mostly. The contract gave her a fair amount of liberty to do her own work; she just couldn't *create* genmod cats for anyone else while under contract, nor did she own any of the genetic research that went into creating the cats Ambré and Hernane kept. And why had Abraham even brought that stupid instance up? Why had she even told him about it when she'd called? When the look on his face said he did not believe her first answer and didn't care about her explanation, Obast felt compelled to continue. "Not really.

And I…probably might have just been overreacting. It was probably nothing." In response to Abraham's continued heavy silence, she added, "Really. It's probably nothing."

"Is it?" The two words weighed more than all the equipment in her lab.

She closed her eyes and did her best not to recall that dance with her advisor…

"Shadi, look at me." He nudged her shoulder. When she looked up, he continued, "I'm your brother. I'm still here for you, no matter what. You know that, right? Even if you weren't making all that money, even if we had to get by taking care of Ma on our income, I'm here for you."

She reached up and kissed both his cheeks. "I know. But I'm also good at taking care of myself, and I don't need you worrying for me. Can we please drop this?"

A long silence said he didn't want to drop it, but he finally agreed. "Only if you stay for dinner." He widened his eyes, giving his best baby brother begging face. "Nebla even made fried okra from the farmer's market to serve over the ful."

Obast couldn't help but laugh. "You know the Smoke Beast stays with me."

"I'm sure we have a can of tuna about to go bad around here somewhere that Nebla might be willing to part with for your monster cat…"

★★★

Why in all the world did they think they needed another cat? Obast lamented as she ran her hand down the nursing kittens. Two fully hypoallergenic Bengalese Rexes with the gorgeous golden coats of whorled stripes. TeeLee hadn't even been a year old when Ambre had started dropping hints. And with success after only three fertilized litters—an incredibly short experimentation period—Ambré and Hernane would be the power couple of the GenMod cat show world with an unprecedented *three* animals. From the look of this litter, three *star quality* show cats.

What would Ambré and Hernane have done if she'd said "no"? She had grounds to do so, based on her contract. But they could dissolve the contract and find another geneticist—keeping all of Obast's work on the three cats for themselves. Keeping their cats.

But seeing the new kittens, not yet ready to take home but looking to be entirely viable, had made Ambré squeal with joy like a teenager and throw herself into Hernane's arms. And seeing the two women happy together was a good sign. Perhaps the earlier affections—Obast now felt fairly certain that they had been purposeful affections—might be over. Most recently—and while Hernane had been in the same room!—Obast had felt the solid warmth of a hand that lingered longer than an accidental brush against her rear. If this kitten made *that* problem go away...if it magically brought peace to her primary clients' household...

Obast knew she ought to be too rational to consider such a far-fetched gamble.

Would you have even said "no" if you thought you could? asked another voice in her head. It was a voice she didn't like, but one that was correct, nonetheless.

Ambré and Herane hadn't *exactly* challenged her to create a more beautiful, fully hypoallergenic cat than their Parisian friends. But they had said that they were sure that, if she thought to put her efforts into it, Obast *could* do so.

Ambré had even spoken to the conceit of Obast's name. "Bast was the Egyptian cat goddess, right?"

"Yes. My father's Egyptian, so I wanted to honor him while I represented myself. And the O is for my mother, who's Irish, and that's a common addition to Irish last names. Together, it means I'm 'of the cat goddess,'" the doctor had explained.

Ambré had doted upon the cleverness of the name, as well as Obast's talents, and before she realized it, her geneticist side was already thinking in productive patterns. And here was a litter with not one but *two* potentially viable kittens.

And she would deliver one of them into a house where there were already two cats visiting her office with increasing frequency, sporting various injuries. Even after almost two years of socializing.

What is wrong with me?

***

I hope you do better at reading contracts than reading people, Ms. Adel.

To this day, Obast figured her veterinary advisor had assumed his last words to her would go over her head. Perhaps they had. No. She'd gone over her contract several times with Hernane, the more business minded of the two.

"Why am I signing over any and all work I do to develop, test, create, and care for the animals you keep as your property?" she'd asked. Even for the money she was being offered—and she'd done well, she felt, in not letting on how much she'd *needed* the money at that time—that was a massive concession and potential loss on her part. "Why isn't a non-disclosure agreement sufficient?"

Hernane had looked her in the eye and said, "Because transferring ownership means if you screw us or use any of your work to aid a competitor or help them make a better cat, it's a *criminal* charge with higher penalties for the loss to our business and welfare." With a slow smile, she'd added, "Really, it's no different than what major corporations ask of their programmers, engineers, and designers. Genetic engineering has become a profitable commodity, my dear."

Of course, as Obast had designed Smokey and TeeLee, she'd discovered several splicing techniques and patterns that had simplified the process and opened doors in working with a variety of feline diseases. Those techniques and application were, of course, a grey area that a good enough lawyer might consider as property of the Okafor-Westin estate. The inability to use those with other potential clients would be a severe handicap.

Not that Obast was thinking of breaking contract. Even with just the two cats, with their other jobs and holdings, Ambré and Hernane could and did pay her better than any other client she would likely find. And despite the contract, she still had a fair amount of freedom and ownership on work she didn't do specifically for them.

With another client, would she have that freedom? Or would they demand more transparency? Want even more documentation about all the "product" that passed through her labs?

Could she even bring herself to continue doing designer geneticist work knowing what she knew?

"I'm not breaking contract," Obast told herself as she checked the mirror once more before Ambré arrived to pick up her kitten. She had never used makeup, always kept her hair back and out of her face, and lived in turtlenecks, trousers, and lab coats. Still, was there a way to make herself look even plainer or more undesirable?

Her hope about whatever was going on between the two women being fixed with the coming arrival of a new kitten had been short lived. Ambré had spent most of the last office visit with one hand on the small of the doctor's back, speaking so close Obast could smell the cucumber mint water on her breath.

Her old advisor, Dr. Mandel Elliot, had smelled of candied fennel seed—he'd always kept a bowl of it in his office—and cigarettes. Though it had been over a decade since she'd last seen the bastard, his scent lingered with the same pungency as the billionaire's refreshment. Why memories she'd banished long ago were resurfacing with razor-sharp clarity was, unfortunately, no mystery to Obast.

The only person she'd fooled with her attempts at naïvely misunderstanding his veiled language and too-familiar touches had been herself. *You're just over-analyzing*, she'd told herself. Until his final comment upon seeing her gape at how low she'd ranked in the veterinary college. So low she'd lost all financial aid for her second doctorate in genetics. Even after achieving top grades in genetics—under a different advisor—her records in veterinary school left her scrambling for the lowest-paying positions after graduation.

Until Ambré and Hernane had seen her work on feline peritonitis through gene therapy and had offered her a contract. They had saved her from the crushing debt she'd accumulated for herself and her family.

Tightening her ponytail to make it look more severe and pull at her temples, Obast hoped Hernane came with Ambré to pick up the kitten. Something going wrong with this contract could be even more ruinous than her advisor's wrath.

***

The night after sending Ambré home with her surviving hypoallergenic kitten, Obast lay flat on her living room floor, flipping the display screens back and forth on her watch phone with half-hearted flicks of her fingers. Projected in front of her eyes from her headband, the image switched between the home page and her brother's number.

Parti had long since stopped batting through the projection and now vibrated a line down Obast's chest and stomach with her purrs. Beba still half-heartedly swatted while she lay on her back, making a furry halo around Obast's head, her silken gold (but not hypoallergenic) fur tangled in the remains of the doctor's black ponytail with every flick of the overlarge kitten's tail. Brat and Scat, soft, adorable, yet seal-pointed rather than spotted and entirely unhypoallergenic, were the youngest two and the last two of Obast's pride of survivors. They had decided to nap, tangled midwrestle, over one of her ankles.

Even surrounded by all her babies, her mind darted to Smokey, concerned about how her first cat was doing. Was she getting along with the newest addition to the Okafor-Westin household? Would there be another emergency visit in the morning? Were all the cats getting the attention they needed?

And then there was the question Obast hadn't wanted to think about. *Why did Ambré think she could kiss me?*

And even worse, *What does this mean for my work? Will she fire me for my reaction?*

And worst of all, *What will happen to the cats without me?*

Obast outright owned the clinic and all of her equipment. She never spent frivolously: no fancy clothes, handbags, shoes, or even entertainment projected into her private network. All her earnings went directly to her family, to paying off mortgages, school loans, and any other debt. And to caring for her cats. She'd been raised frugally; she knew how to save. If Ambré and Hernane wished to dissolve their contract with Obast, it would be difficult, but not impossible. If they were to speak against her, though, and if she were to lose her accreditation as a veterinary geneticist for the genmod breeders...

Well, she could always turn this into a regular veterinary practice. It wouldn't be impossible.

If they didn't try and get her barred from all veterinary

work…

More importantly…what would become of Smokey, TeeLee, and Sunny—

Sunny. Had she even had a chance to tell Ambré about the surviving kitten's nickname?

And…what if they reported Smokey's temper? The fact she'd attacked a human? That would be the end of the Smoke Beast!

Perhaps Ambré was just exceptionally excited for Sunny, Obast argued to herself, though neither TeeLee nor Smokey had elicited such a response. *Why today? Why now?*

Yesterday, she'd informed Ambré and Hernane that there was still no sign of the heart irregularity that had killed Sunny's sister a week ago. She'd come down and found the poor thing dead; she hoped the kitten's passing had been painless.

Even then, Ambré had been impatient to take the other kitten home, pouting against the *extra* week of observation Obast had insisted upon for the surviving kitten.

When she'd called this morning to inform the couple that the observation time was up, Ambré had demanded the earliest appointment available to come and get the kitten.

Though she could have adjusted her appointments, Obast had made Ambré wait until after lunch. Upon seeing the woman's girlish delight in cuddling the kitten, Obast hadn't been able to stop smiling. In that moment, she'd even forgotten the woman's unwanted affections. For Ambré, that first moment she held a kitten—*her kitten*—was pure magic. That was how the woman had described it.

And then, after a short-for-Ambré cuddle with the kitten, she'd put it in a tiny fancy carrier, turned, and kissed Obast.

On the lips.

After that, Obast's memory failed her. There was a blur and Ambré leaving very quickly with the kitten, beautifully gold with whorls and spots of the deepest black. Hypoallergenic *and* already repeating words.

Feeling capsized from the storm of human interaction that day, Obast thought upon the cats—the creatures she understood best.

The prior day, she'd seen Smokey and TeeLee for Smokey's daily checkup and shot and TeeLee's weekly checkup. There continued to be a marked increase in use and selection of naughty words that opened each visit, particularly from Smokey. The older cat also had shown heightened blood pressure and stress indicators that didn't seem to come from any physical ailments. TeeLee had performed a growing vocabulary of similar ilk—though that could come from hearing her big sister. She, too, had displayed elevated vitals and stress indicators compared to when she was still living in the lab. Both cats were kept in separate parts of the house now, so there were fewer fights, yet both regularly showed up with minor injuries: scratches, bruises. Seen through the eyes of the cats—even without what had been happening with Ambré—Obast regretfully concluded there were more than a few troubles in their home life.

The veterinary geneticist dismissed her contact list and flipped away the display hologram, letting her arm flop to the side in defeat.

What *could* she tell her brother if she called him? And what could he even do to help?

Nothing was the answer. She'd figure something out. For now, she had a job to do for her own feline goddesses— provide offerings of snuggles and playtime.

Clearing her mind as she'd cleared her holographic display, she rearranged the cats and rolled to her belly, snatching a ribbon from under the couch. With a catlike grin of her own, she waggled it for her little ones.

***

Her wrist tablet phone was ringing.

Obast blinked groggily, wondering why she felt so stiff and sore before she realized she was still on the floor, all four cats either on top of or against her. Her sun sensors only lit the house for dawn—this time of year, nearly an hour before she'd normally awake.

The *brrring*ing buzz made her jump, eliciting several displeased looks and vocalizations, which made her feel badly—despite the fact her cats were basically using her as warm furniture. She managed to free her wrist tablet and perform the proper flicking and gesturing to send up the display without even looking at the number. Her phone was already set to disable video and block any noise not her voice; what if an auditor or another gen-vet called and heard or saw one of her creations she'd logged as dead?

"Doctor Obast, we're almost at the clinic. We need you right away." Hernane's voice sounded panicked; Hernane never panicked.

"O-of course, I'll be right down. What's—" The call disconnected before she could ask for details.

Going over all the worst case scenarios in her head, Obast gathered her house pride to lock in their rooms lest anyone visit during the day. Parti, sleeping on her chest, was easy. She also managed to scoop up Scat as the cat blinked to adjust to the motion-brightened lighting. She caught a confused Beba before she was awake enough to run, but still had to chase the appropriately named Brat to get her into her kennel. After a sloppy dump of food in their bowls, Obast cleaned herself up to the best of her ability.

She was still snapping an elastic around her bun when she opened the doors for Hernane and Ambré.

Both women were smeared with blood.

Obast started from the shock of such a sight. Ambré, cradling a bundle of bloodied cloth in her arms, shouldered her way in and started heading for the main examination room without saying a word.

Hernane at least looked at Obast, her pupils barely pinpricks in her blue-grey eyes. "We need your help. Please."

"Of course." Pulling herself together, Obast opened up the exam room

Ambré shoved by the doctor again and started gently laying out the rags. As she did so, Obast saw heartbreak and fury streaming out of her topaz eyes and flowing down her cheeks.

"*Oh!*" Obast gasped at what she saw.

"You can save them, right?" Hernane asked.

"Save them! Use your genetic whatevers and fancy doctorates and *save* them," Ambré ordered.

Obast slowly shook her head as she approached the table. Her ability to play a god only covered creating the cats' lives. With a torn breath, she brushed her finger over TeeLee's tiny, twisted, gaping throat. No, of course there was no pulse. When she tried to find Sunny's heartbeat, a small gush of blood rivered out from gashes across the kitten's abdomen, soaking into the towel.

Her brain knew there was nothing she could do; the trauma was too great for cats so small, so young. Their skin and bones were delicate; there was only so much blood each could lose. Still, she spun through all possible treatments…

Ambré's chastisement sounded far away. "Do something! Why aren't you doing anything? Save them!"

Hernane's words could not be made out, but her tone was soothing, though ragged. Like the wounds on the little kittens.

Swallowing a burning in her throat, Obast tucked the towel around the two kitten bodies, hands shaking. "I'm sorry," she whispered.

"You're sorry? You're *sorry*?!" Ambré lunged at the doctor, who didn't even flinch. Hernane caught her in arms, apparently stronger than her slender size would suggest.

"Your monster was shut up in her own room. She opened the goddamned door and *hunted* them!"

Despite the towel covering their broken bodies, Obast could picture them both—how they moved, how they'd grown, how they'd spoken. She also imagined Smokey, crying through the door for attention, growing angrier. Could she have opened a door? Sphynx and Siamese cats were known for their dexterity—and the breeds were chosen for their intellect.

"I will destroy you!" Ambré yowled in fury. "You will *never* touch another cat again in your *life*, you fucking bitch! I will *end* you!"

Hernane, sobbing herself, pulled Ambré from the room. No clients or patients would be waiting yet; they wouldn't see, wouldn't hear. Perhaps one or two of her staff had come in early, but Obast would have to speak to them all anyway.

A cold voice in the doctor's head, however, could not help but ask: Upon looking at the towel-shrouds, were the two women seeing millions of dollars in lost investments? Would that account for their emotional displays?

No…She couldn't believe that. Despite everything, Obast preferred to think that the women mourned, as she did, the loss of two beautiful lives.

Sorrow made all animals act unnaturally.

***

Obast called in all three of her technicians to cover the

rest of the day. She had to focus on the report she must file. She dare not let herself think of what would follow. The techs knew this was serious and she was not to be disturbed unless there were life-threatening circumstances; they did not know she also gave the order so they wouldn't see her crying.

Unfortunately, she did not remain alone for long. Not an hour after Ambré and Hernane had left, Ambré was back with Smokey hissing cusses from her carrier.

"Doctor, I'm sorry—but Ms. Okafor will only see you," squeaked Marisa, one of the office staff, through the cracked door.

"Of course. I'll be right out." After splashing some cold water on her face and patting it dry, Obast headed back to the lobby on jelly knees.

Ambré's eyes were amber ice. "We cannot have a killer animal in the house."

Obast wanted to spit back that the woman should have done better to integrate the cats, that she and Hernane had been given specific instructions on how to handle highly intelligent creatures. Perhaps, if they'd not been so preoccupied with scores and awards, with whatever problems were happening between them, the two women could have noticed and addressed problems as they arose.

But she said nothing. The law was explicit that any genmod animal that attacked would be put down, their genetic material destroyed, and their mods erased from all private and business records—except for what needed to be submitted to the Federal Department of Genetic Modification for research, of course. Regardless of the circumstances.

Obast had believed that something like this would never happen. After all, Smokey had been a part of Ambré and Hernane's life for almost six years now.

Yet, as Ambré thrust the carrier at her, there was no pause. No tender look.

"Of course, we expect a *full* audit of your facility before you create another genmod animal," she said, then narrowed her eyes to knife-slits. "That is, if their findings don't *bar* you from all further work in genetic modification." Then she raised her voice ever so slightly so it was clearly audible to the few patients in the lobby. "Assuming they don't bar you from working with *any* other animal. Just to be sure."

Obast rarely swore, but she very much appreciated Smokey's "*ucking hitch hoowhagss*" commentary. If it were to be the poor cat's last words, at least they were appropriate. Even if their target turned on her heel and left unfazed.

Slowly, deliberately, Obast lifted the carrier, opened it with one hand, and started stroking Smokey's head. "I'm sorry your humans treated you so poorly that you had to act out just to get their attention." She turned and headed down the hall, straight for the closed lab, letting the humans in the lobby decide for themselves if they wished to leave or stay.

It gave her the smallest sense of smug comfort that the vet technicians continued to be busy for the rest of the day.

★★★

Obast had not locked Smokey in quarantine as was protocol. Instead, she'd put her in one of her house kennels, thinking it'd be more comfortable than the lab. It was removed from the other cats, whom she'd also secured into their kennels, just to be safe.

She'd questioned her decision when the Smoke Beast started growling and hissing her angry commentary as soon as she started to walk away. She returned to the cat three times to assure her she was loved and would be more comfortable here instead of the lab. She even tried bribery. "Look, your favorite treats. Here's a big bowl of them."

Eventually, Obast had to leave. She locked herself in her office to finish filing the needed information for the Department of Genetic Modification. And while she was meticulous in her legal wording and citation, a part of her mind was not at all on the forms in front of her.

A part wasn't even thinking in *legal* parameters.

★★★

Obast smelled blood when she opened her apartment door. Smokey greeted her, purring. Blood speckled red on her silky silver fur and dark skin.

"Oh no. Nonono!" Hopping over the Smoke Beast— Beast!—she ran to her kennel room. Two kitty voices mewled, shaking with terrified purrs. Smokey flew by Obast, but the doctor caught her. While the cat spat and hissed her vulgarities, Obast was well aware of how little her sharp claws scratched. If nothing else, Smokey didn't want to hurt *her*. She pressed the cat into a tight, full body embrace. Then with a practiced maneuver, she secured the Smoke Beast into a squeeze carrier.

After wrapping the carrier in her blankets and comforter—she hoped her scent would comfort the cat— Obast returned to the kennels. She had secured Smokey in the separate kennel, locked it, and shut the room door. She was certain of it; she hadn't wanted to take any chances.

She knew better than anyone that three of the smartest, most dexterous cats' genes had gone into her first baby.

The door to Scat and Brat's shared kennel was open. All their play-fighting hadn't prepared them for an actual attack. As the newest creations, they'd been engineered more docile than prior litters.

No pulse on either, no breathing, and too much blood.

She covered them with their blanket.

Had she created a monster? Quite literally through genetics? Or was it Ambré's and Hernane's treatment that had pushed the cat over the edge? Had Smokey associated neglect and abuse with any and all other cats?

Neither Beba's nor Parti's doors were open. Blood spots rusted Beba's golden face and crusted both front paws. Obast pulled her from the kennel and looked for injuries. Three toe pads were almost ripped off, and blood trickled sickeningly from both feet. She wrapped them with a blanket for the time being and headed to the bathroom linen closet where she kept her medical supplies.

The FDGM inspectors and representatives would arrive in the morning. They would destroy every embryo, every piece of reproductive material, every "product" of her studies.

And they would search her private quarters. Someone might already be auditing her work, finding discrepancies between the "unviable product" she filed and the dead matter she'd actually sent in.

They would not handle her creations kindly; the cats' lives would end with uncaring hands and tests and needles. The bodies would likely all be sent for dissection and then destruction. There would be no lovely garden for eternity.

If they had to die, it would be by *her* hand. The hand of the one who'd created them, who loved them. She would secretly bury their bodies among flowers and face whatever fines or consequences they threw at her.

This—*this*…situation…was not the quiet, gentle euthanasia she'd designed.

Leaning against the cold, tiled bathroom wall, Obast slid to the floor, cradling the bleeding, mewing Beba. She kissed her soft head over and over, rubbing her chin across the cat's face. Feeling with her hand because she couldn't see through tears, she worked through the collection of syringes in her coat pocket—enough for all of them. Two were dead by Smokey's claws; three deserved to be given gentle repose.

Obast found the right syringe. First the sedative. Then the barbiturate. She didn't know how long she held Beba after administering the shots—it felt like hours—but she finally lost all vitals.

Now for Parti.

Parti hissed. No words—just pure emotion. She'd be able to smell Beba's death on Obast. Even so, she did not fight when Obast gathered her. She brought the cat to the couch where they'd often cuddled with a book. She didn't bother to look for injuries. Hugging the ball of purrs and hisses, Obast slipped in the sedative needle. When Parti became limp weight, the doctor dosed her with the barbiturate. After half an hour, the cat still breathed. Obast pulled out a second barbiturate needle, weeping. Parti didn't want to die; she wasn't giving up. It took a third dose...

How her hands still worked, Obast did not know. How she stood, shrouded Parti in a bright towel, and then walked to her bedroom door was further a mystery. Turning the knob stopped her.

No, not the knob. The voice crying behind the door.

"*Okter. Okter. Okter Owasss. Okter Owass...Okter Sshaardrdia.*"

"Oh!" She sobbed more, collapsing on the doorframe, clutching the syringes to her mouth. Smokey was calling. Calling her name. Doctor. Obast. Doctor Shadia. She knew the cat's language; she understood.

And she couldn't.

Shoving the unopened needles back into her lab coat pocket, Obast released Smokey from the squeeze carrier, held the cat to her chest, and threw herself on the bed. She cried, not caring that she smelled of urine and blood. Smokey settled against her, purring and adjusting herself to clean Obast's chin. Wiping her face on the pillow, Obast made herself move again.

There was very little time and an awful lot to do.

***

"Shadia, what in the world are you doing out here?"

She looked at Abraham. Of course he would have heard her. It was probably for the better. Perhaps she should have called…

"I am digging graves."

"I can see that. Why are you digging graves in the garden in the middle of the night? What's wrong?"

"It's not the middle of the night," she corrected as she continued digging. In the dim light of her tablet-watch, she piled the dirt separately from the root balls of flowers she'd dug up earlier. "It is the darkest hours before dawn. And I have four dead cats that deserve to spend eternity in gardens. The Gardens of New Bubastis. Perhaps you could plant some catnip? I recall learning it was good for human muscle cramps and headaches…"

Abraham grabbed her shoulders, making her stop. "Talk to me, Shadi. You're scaring me."

For a moment, she moved her mouth without words, and then the story poured out. She found herself leaning her head on his shoulders and rubbing fresh tears and snot on her brother's bathrobe. She waited for her baby brother to scold her, to plead why she hadn't called him sooner, to demand to know what her plan was now.

He did none of these things. Planting a kiss on the top of her head, he let her go and headed to the shed. With his own shovel, he dug beside her.

After minutes of silent digging, Obast said, "I gave all

the techs and receptionists two years' worth of wages. And I put half of what remained into Mom's account for you. But I figured I'd need cash."

"You're going on the run?"

"At first...I'd thought...I'd thought I'd just let myself get taken to jail. I was going to kill all of them, all my babies, gently, before they...before they *slaughtered* them all. I-I'd expose what happens to the not-star-quality genmod cats, and...and how people treat the 'stars' like... like designer accessories—not the sentient creatures they are. Worthy of dignity, love, and respect. Maybe if I did that..."

Abraham swallowed.

Obast responded to his unspoken question. "But people were doing this...this pet designing...this... dehumanizing isn't the right word, but-but *that*...long before genmod shows. What would I change? And there's Smokey..."

"What do you need?" Abraham asked.

Obast paused. "Tell Mom...I love her, always, and that I fell in love." Of course her brother knew the last part was a lie, but he didn't argue. She continued, "That will make her happy; she always worried about me. Tell her...it was with a rival to my employers. We broke laws to be together...ran off, eloped." She chuckled, wiping her nose on her filthy labcoat. "Make it like one of her romance novels, the collection she kept hidden under her shoes."

"Nebla reads them to her now. A few chapters a day." Abraham sniffled. "Where will you go? Can you even tell me?"

"Several European countries are against genmod designer pets..." Obast pulled the four shrouded cats from her cooler duffel. Earlier that night, she'd given Smokey an oral sedative treat—she couldn't stomach handling another needle—so the Beast was asleep in her carrier below an azalea bush.

"Mostly cold ones. You hate the cold," Abraham said.

"So will Smokey; I altered her hormones. She's going to lose all her fur. I can't be seen with the world's most decorated genmod cat. We'll keep each other warm." After a moment staring at the wrapped bodies, she placed each one in the large hole.

Abraham helped refill the grave and replant the flowers.

Smokey was waking and beginning to chirp. "*Hoordr? Hirrer?*"

"What's she saying?"

"Food. Dinner." Glancing at the sky, Obast added, "I need to go. I've got a friend with a plane waiting for me."

"*Hrdoordra.*"

When Abraham gave the cat a look, Obast translated, "Tuna. I think she was rather fond of that about-to-go-bad tuna."

"I have more. Nebla is the one who eats it, but she buys in bulk," Abraham said. "I'll be quick."

Obast placed Smokey on some loose dirt, hoping that would be enough for her to relieve herself. It was. She picked up the cat and held it to her chest, she felt her purr, "*Oowrwasssrr…Orkrrrr…Oowrwassrr.*"

Was it mimicry? Certainly the cat had heard people say her name. But was it more?

Abraham had come out and paused to stare. "It sounds like she's trying to say Doctor Obast."

Obast nodded. "When I was about to…" She motioned sticking a needle. "She…that's when I couldn't."

"Are you actually going to keep your name? On the run?"

Obast sighed. "I created—*perfected*—whole breeds of

cat with the building blocks of life. And then I destroyed all but one. If that's not the work of a cat goddess, I don't know what is."

Her brother's judgmental tone edged once more. "You don't sound particularly humbled."

"I hurt and I mourn and I wish it turned out differently," she said. Would a cat goddess feel humility? She tucked the Smoke Beast into the carrier with the opened vaccu-seal tuna pouch. "Abraham…Thank you. I love you, baby brother."

"Love you, too, big sis." He hugged her and she felt his tears. "I promise to take care of your Gardens of New Bubastis."

She kissed him once more before running to her rental vehicle. Secure in the carrier, Smokey was purr-speaking again.

"*Oowass…Ordrass…Owass…Ordrass.*"

In the cat's speech, saying "Obast" sounded a lot like trying to say "goddess."

ACKNOWLEDGMENTS

Where Monsters Pray wouldn't exist without the love and support of so many more people than I can properly thank in an "Acknowledgements" section. The stories and poems within these pages have been critiqued, edited, read, and honed by many fantastic editors, writing colleagues, and friends over many years —decades even! So, let me start with a massive and heartfelt "Thank you!" to the many of you who have been my "writing fam" over the years.

Of course, more literally, *Where Monsters Pray* would not only not exist but not be such a perfect rendition of what I could dream without the faith, support, love, and hard work of Michael Takeda and Pink Narcissus Press. From agreeing to print a collection of both fiction and poetry to providing the most perfect cover and art—I still get teary looking at it all!—Michael has gone well above and beyond what I could have hoped for this dark collection of weird, queer, and heartfelt terror.

I also want to thank Rob Smales for being the fantastic copy editor that he is! I have learned a lot in working with you in the many projects. I never expected (though I probably should have!) to have found a wonderful family of loving and supportive friends, colleagues, mentors, and cheerleaders in the horror community—particularly the New England Horror Writers (helmed by the magnanimous Scott Goudsward); Camp Necon where you can get fantastic writing and publishing advice along with some of the best hugs; Christopher Golden and James A. Moore, who set great examples of what it means to be a positive force through darkness; and many more of you who have cheered not only me, but so many other writers along the way.

I thank my parents for always believing I could be whomever or whatever I wanted when I grow up (whenever that may be). And last, but furthest from least, I am eternally grateful for my husband-of-awesome, Scott Wooldridge, who got me into horror as a genre, has always had my back, taken care of me during the always-rocky path of publishing, and has been my most beloved and best friend.

Thank you everyone! I love you!

ABOUT THE AUTHOR

Trisha J. Wooldridge (child-friendly: T.J. Wooldridge) is an award-winning pan-genre, pan-media chaos word witch. Find her in the Shirley Jackson Award-winning *The Twisted Book of Shadows*; some *HWA Poetry Showcase* volumes; all the NEHW anthologies (that she didn't edit); *Don't Turn Out the Lights: A Tribute to Alvin Schwartz's Scary Stories to Tell in the Dark*; *Pseudopod* podcast; and *34 Orchard* literary journal. She's currently releasing the 5-book The Princess and the Dragon cycle, part of The 27 Kingdoms fantasy series from New Mythology Press. *Where Monsters Pray* is her first collection. She also lovingly tortures consenting authors with her editing talents. She spends mystical "free time" with a very patient Husband-of-Awesome; a tiny witch and large witcher kitty pair; a rescued bay gelding; and a matronly calico mare. If you see her at one of the many conventions she haunts, ask if she has her Tarot —and if she'll give you a reading. www.anovelfriend.com.

OTHER TITLES AVAILABLE
FROM PINK NARCISSUS PRESS

INKWEED + THE MELLIFICATION

Two novellas by Nat Buchbinder
"Buchbinder debuts with an inventive and intimate duo of queer, fantastical novellas bound by a common theme of escape from oppressive communities supposedly designed for their denizens' protection [...] There's lots to chew on here." — *Publishers Weekly*

DAUGHTERS OF ICARUS

An anthology of new feminist spec fic
"Throughout, the authors explore themes of gender, identity, and autonomy, with characters as diverse as miniature clones, stripper vampires, aggressive mermaids, and mystical crones. Many of the stories focus on gender roles and the pull of relationships, whether parental, familial, or romantic, among all kinds of people." —*Library Journal*

THE SILENCE OF THE WILTING SKIN

A novella by Tlotlo Tsamaase
Lambda Literary Award Finalist
Nommo Award Finalist
"Motswana author Tsamaase debuts with a lyrical and incisive allegory about personal identity and cultural loss set in an unnamed, phantasmagoric African city. Through magnetic prose, dream logic, and lush imagery, Tsamaase delivers a fierce political message." —*Publishers Weekly* (starred review)

Printed in the USA
CPSIA information can be obtained
at www.ICGtesting.com
LVHW011303260624
783767LV00005B/19